'The people are real and not only
Mary Ann is vital . . . Her school
friends are all full of character and
good talk. The author knows the
locality and the people she writes
about . . . And she has a salty touch
that prevents sentimentality. Mary
Ann mends a good deal of grown-up
trouble . . .'
                                    — *Vanity Fair*

'The character drawing is excellent,
Mary Ann herself is a real joy, and
one senses the truth of the
background.'
                    — *The Times Literary Supplement*

Catherine Cookson

Love and Mary Ann

CORGI BOOKS
A DIVISION OF TRANSWORLD PUBLISHERS LTD
A NATIONAL GENERAL COMPANY

LOVE AND MARY ANN

A CORGI BOOK 0 552 09074 3

First published in Great Britain by
Macdonald & Co. (Publishers) Ltd.

PRINTING HISTORY
Macdonald edition published 1961
Macdonald edition reprinted 1967
Corgi edition published 1972

Corgi Books are published by Transworld
Publishers Ltd.,
Cavendish House, 57–59 Uxbridge Road,
Ealing, London W.5.

Made and printed in Great Britain by
Cox & Wyman Ltd., London, Reading and Fakenham

NOTE: The Australian price appearing on the
back cover is the recommended retail price.

To Sarah and Jack

CONTENTS

CHAPTER ONE

A RIVAL

He stands at the corner
And whistles me out,
With his hands in his pockets
And his shirt hanging out.
But still I love him—
Can't deny it—
I'll be with him
Wherever he goes.

MARY ANN hitched and skipped as she sang. It would seem that she was entertaining the field of sheep, but all except one, a weak-kneed lamb, appeared oblivious to her prancing. Coming to the end of her ditty, she began again as she had done at least ten times already, and she waved the empty feeding-bottle high above her head as she continued her capering, and the lamb, thinking this was but a prelude to another feed from this two-legged mother of his, gambolled with her.

She had reached the elevating line which ended, 'And his shirt hanging out', when she gave an extraordinarily high leap and swung round in mid-air as a voice bellowed above her, 'Stop that!'

When she reached the ground she stared wide-eyed for a second at the old man standing beyond the gate, and then she exclaimed in high glee, 'Why, you're back.'

She scampered the few yards to the gate and climbed on to the bottom rung and looked up into the thin, wrinkled face of Mr. Lord, and again she exclaimed, 'Why, you're back.'

And then she added, 'They're not expecting you afore next week. Me mother was going up to the house the night to see Ben about the spring cleaning. . . .'

'TO . . . NIGHT.'

She swallowed but kept her eyes unblinkingly on him as she repeated dutifully, 'Tonight.' Oh, lordy, he wasn't going to start already, was he?

She smiled broadly at him now, a smile of welcome, for she was truly pleased to see him, and to take his mind off the obsession for good grammar she held up the empty feeding-bottle and, thumbing down towards the lamb which was now nibbling at the wire-netting covering the gate, she said, 'I feed Penelope. He thinks I'm his ma . . . mother. His mother died and me da said if I fed him . . . I mean fed it . . . her – it's a her – he would let me keep her and not send her away.'

She continued to look up at him, waiting for him to make some comment. She knew that she had said da instead of father, but it was no use, she couldn't call her da her father; she'd had that out with Mr. Lord a long time ago.

'What were you singing?'

'Eh?'

'Eh!'

'I'm sorry, I mean pardon.' She dropped her eyes away from him now. Oh, he was ratty. And just come back from a month's holiday. She had missed him, but she'd also missed his chastising.

'I asked you a question.'

'I don't know what it's called really, I think it might be "Whistle an' I'll come to ye, me lad", but it goes, "He stands at the corner and whistles me out . . ."'

'I heard how it went. Do they teach you that at school?'

'No.'

'Where did you hear it then?'

Her head moved around as if she were casually observing the flock of sheep. She knew if she spoke the truth and said 'From Corny, Mrs. McBride's grandson' he would know she had been going to Burton Street and Mulhattan's Hall and he had told her mother that she shouldn't be allowed to go there, that all those old associations should be dropped. Her mother had tactfully refrained from stating her opinion on this matter, but later on, when her da had found out, he had said, 'She's going to Fanny's when she wants to', to which her mother had replied, 'He didn't really mean Fanny in particular. I suppose he was thinking that if she went there she would meet up with Sarah Flannagan and there would be the usual fighting in the street. It was that he was likely thinking about.' But her da had said flatly again, 'She can go to Mulhattan's Hall whenever the fancy takes her.' And then he had added, 'Don't you start trying to alter her, Liz; there's enough working along that line with the old boy; he's an educational establishment in himself.'

So, knowing the way the wind blew, Mary Ann was forced to fib. 'I heard a comic on the wireless singing it.' She turned her head to look at him to see if he believed her. . . . He didn't.

'Come along.'

She went to climb over the gate when his bark hit her again. 'Mary Ann!'

She got slowly down from the third bar of the gate, lifted the heavy latch, pushed the lamb away from following her, closed the gate again, then looked at him.

'You're a big girl now, you shouldn't have to be told to walk through a gate instead of over it.'

She continued to look at him. You didn't know how to take the things he said. He had called her a big girl, when just before he went on his holidays he had said to her mother, 'We must get her to do special exercises, she's not growing as she should.' She did not point out to him that she was always doing exercises to make herself taller, such as hanging from the lower boughs of trees and fixing her feet in the rails of the bed and trying from there to reach the window-sill, which even at the nearest remained two feet away. One day she had been over the moon when the distance had cut itself in half, only to find after some observation that it was the bed that had moved. She knew she was little; she didn't like being little, but she would rather be little than do any more exercises – Mr. Lord's kind of exercises, anyway, for they were sure to turn out to be some form of motion that she didn't like. He usually made her do things that she didn't like.

'Where's everybody?'

They were walking along the road now towards the farm, and Mary Ann realized that this question at least was not out of order, for there was not a soul to be seen. She could see the farm-house, which was their house, along the road to the left, and there was no sign of anyone near it. And still to the left, away up the hill, nearly at the top, opulent in its newness and dominating in its position, was Mr. Lord's house. And there wasn't a soul to be seen near that either. The sloping garden was all ablaze with daffodils, tulips and the first azaleas, and presented a magnificent sight, and she drew his attention to it, saying, 'Look, isn't the garden bonnie? They weren't out when you left.'

Mr. Lord cast his eyes up the hill and he let them rest there for a moment before he said, 'Where's Tony?'

The house and the garden had reminded him of his grandson, if he needed reminding, and she realized, if she hadn't done so before, that he was in a paddy. He was always in a paddy when he spoke Tony's name like that, sharp, as if Tony was committing a crime for not being within sight. It was just over three years ago that Mr. Lord discovered he had a grandson at all, and her da had said then, and often since, that he wouldn't be in Tony's shoes for all the tea in China, for Tony now couldn't call his soul his own, and it was as well for him that he was learning to run the managing side of the shipyard, for if he had remained on the farm, as he had really wanted to do, he wouldn't have been able to get out of the old man's sight to draw breath. That's what her da said. She liked Tony . . . oh, she did. When she grew up she was going to marry him and have three boys and three girls. The boys were going to be called Peter, James and John like the Apostles, and the girls were going to be called Mary, Martha and Elizabeth like those in the Bible history, and they would all live in Mr. Lord's house on the hill, and they would have a television.

There was no television on the farm at all. It was one of the few things that her da and Mr. Lord seemed to agree about. Mr. Lord said it was . . . What was that word? A long word . . . like mortal sin . . . demoralizing. Yes, that was it – he thought it was demoralizing. And her father wouldn't hear of television in the house because of Michael and her having to do their homework. And he, too, did homework – well, sort of, for he was always reading up books about cows and bullocks and all the things they could catch. Her mother said that if she had known that animals could catch so many diseases she would never have eaten meat in the first place, but now she supposed it was too late to bother.

'Has everybody been wiped out by a plague or something? . . . .Shaughnessy!'

They were standing in the yard now.

'It's no use shouting for me da, he's not there. He's gone into Jarrow, to the wharf, about some timber. Him and Tony. Tony's driving the lorry because he hadn't to go into the office this morning, and our Michael went with them to help load.'

Mr. Lord looked down on her. He stared down on her, and she did not know if it was because she had said him and Tony went, instead of Tony and he, or that he was vexed at her da and Tony going off together. She knew he didn't like Tony spending so much time in their house and talking to her da.

Three years ago, when Mr. Lord had been very ill and unable to do much shouting, everything on the farm had been lovely. But since he had got better he had gone around looking for trouble. You always knew he was well when he shouted; he only talked quietly if he was bad or very angry about something. In a way she preferred his shouting. And now he shouted at Mr. Johnson, who was coming out of the cowshed.

'Is everybody asleep around here?'

Mr. Johnson came quickly towards him. He was a biggish man, and thick with it, and he was always smiling, and Mary Ann didn't like him. Her mother said Mr. Johnson's smile was smarmy, and she supposed that was why she didn't like him. She didn't like any of the Johnsons – Mr. Johnson, Mrs. Johnson or their Lorna. Lorna worked in Newcastle in an office and thought herself the last word. She was always wearing something different and whenever she could she talked to Tony. . . . This was the main reason why she didn't like Lorna. The reason why she didn't like Mrs. Johnson was because her ma didn't care for Mrs. Johnson. Every time Mrs. Johnson talked to her ma she was always telling her what a wonderful worker Mr. Johnson was and how clever he was with animals, and how highly everybody thought of her daughter. Her mother said she talked as if Lorna had just to raise her finger and all the men in Newcastle would fall on their knees.

'Oh, it is nice to see you back, sir. And how're you feeling? Have you enjoyed your holiday?'

Mr. Lord did not return Mr. Johnson's beaming smile, nor answer his kind inquiries, but asked abruptly, 'Where's everybody? Jones? Len?'

'Well now, well now.' Mr. Johnson pursed his mouth and made a motion with his fingers as if to pluck his lips off his face. 'Jones . . . well, Jones is down in the bottom meadow, Mr. Lord; he went down there half an hour gone. And Len . . . Len is mixing meal in the store-room at this minute. As for the boss—' Here Mr. Johnson paused. 'Well, he's taken a trip, as far as I know, into Newcastle.'

'He hasn't. He's gone to Jarrow to see about some timber.'

Mary Ann looked up into Mr. Johnson's now unsmiling face, and, turning her gaze on Mr. Lord, she said, 'He hasn't gone into Newcastle. He's gone to Jarrow, as I told you.'

Mr. Lord did not answer her, nor Mr. Johnson, he just looked at the man before turning away. And Mary Ann looked at Mr. Johnson before she, too, turned away. That's the kind of thing Mr. Johnson did. . . . A trip into Newcastle. It was just as if her da had gone off on a jaunt. Oh, she didn't like the Johnsons.

Mr. Lord was now striding towards the farm-house, and Mary Ann hoped fervently that her mother would have some coffee ready and would ask Mr. Lord to sit down and have a cup and he would get over his temper. As she made her wish she drew a quick pattern of the Sacred Heart on her flat chest. And, as often before when she had made this magic sign, her wish was granted, for her mother had just made some fresh coffee, and it was in the new percolator her da had bought at Christmas.

Her mother's face was flushed because she had been at the oven turning some scones. She always looked bonnier when her face was flushed; it set off her blonde hair and made her look like a young girl again. Her ma had got bonnier and bonnier this last three years. And she had some nice clothes an' all, not like Lorna Johnson's flashy things, but nice.

Lizzie Shaughnessy turned to her husband's employer with a sincere warm greeting, saying, 'Oh, Mr. Lord, I'm glad to see you. Come in and sit down.' And when he was sitting by the kitchen table she said tactfully, 'We weren't expecting you so soon, but,' she added quickly, 'nevertheless it's good to see you. I didn't hear the car.'

'No, I had a puncture coming out of Pellet's Lane. I left it there.' And now his thin shoulders went back and he looked at her as if she was in some way responsible for the farm appearing deserted, for his voice was harsh as he said, 'And here I come home and not a soul to be seen.'

'Mike's gone for some timber, Mr. Lord. The others are about at their work.'

'Yes, yes, so I understand.' He flapped his hand at her. 'But that's not all. . . . I'm annoyed, Mrs. Shaughnessy, not so much about the place being deserted, but about this one here.' He put out his arm and indicated Mary Ann.

Lizzie looked at her daughter, her own face expressionless. What had she done now? Mary Ann's indignant countenance was telling her quite plainly that in her own opinion she had done nothing, nothing to merit Mr. Lord's censure. Lizzie knew that Mr. Lord's censure was always for Mary Ann's own good, but, oh, it could be trying to everybody. He had this bee firmly fixed in his bonnet about moulding her into a little lady. Well, everything was being done to this end. Her daughter was attending the best convent school in the county, she was mixing with the better-class children of Newcastle and Durham and thereabouts, but . . . Lizzie paused on the but. Was there any noticeable impression of all this on Mary Ann? Her school reports said that she was making good progress in all subjects, particularly English. At school Mary

Ann evidently proved to the teachers that she was making good progress, and when in company and on her best behaviour Lizzie herself had evidence of it, but once she was on the farm and running loose she seemed to revert back to the child she had always been. English and grammar had become the bugbear of their lives – she wished she could take Mike's view and laugh at it. Mike was all for Mary Ann being educated; he was paying for her school fees himself, not allowing Mr. Lord to spend a penny on her, yet at the same time she knew that her husband took a covert delight in that the convent polish was not adhering to his daughter. Mary Ann, like her father, was an individual. She wished at times she wasn't so much of an individual. Yet she knew that if it hadn't been for her daughter's character she wouldn't at this moment be in this kitchen, happy as she had never been in her life before, nor would Mike be in the position of manager of a farm, with a bank-book behind him and a settled future before him. Everything they had they owed to this child and her individuality. Had she been other than she was Mr. Lord would have passed her by. It was because they had one particular trait in common that he was attracted to her; the trait of tenacity. Mary Ann's tenacity had taken the form of working towards her father's security, and because of her tenacity in this direction she had captivated Mr. Lord. The Lord as she had called him until recently.

Never was a man, Lizzie thought, so well named, for he was not only lord of all he surveyed, he was lord of all their lives; particularly was he lord of her daughter's life. Deep within her she was aware that Mary Ann's destiny lay in his hands. She did not express this view to Mike, for it would have aroused his anger. Three years ago, when Mr. Lord had acquired a grandson, he had on the surface relinquished his deep interest in Mary Ann, but Lizzie knew the letting go was only on the surface; he was as determined as ever to shape her life. She said quietly, 'What has she done?'

'She was entertaining the cattle with a bawdy song.'

'A bawdy song?' Lizzie looked at Mary Ann, and Mary Ann, her small mouth drawn into a tight line, turned cold, accusing eyes on Mr. Lord. Bawdy meant nasty. Well, whatever it meant, 'He stands at the corner' wasn't that kind of song. She snapped her eyes from him up to her mother and said primly, 'It wasn't. I was only singing "He stands at the corner".'

Lizzie lowered her eyes for a moment before looking at Mr. Lord. She knew 'He stands at the corner', she knew it as a child, but she had never heard Mary Ann singing it and she didn't know where she had picked it up. Certainly not from anyone in the house.

'Do you know this song?'

'I . . .' Lizzie hesitated. 'I heard it years ago. It's a very old song.'

'And in my opinion most unsuitable for a child.'

There followed an uncomfortable silence until Lizzie asked, 'Can I get you a cup of coffee, I've just made it?'

'Yes. Yes, thank you.'

Mary Ann sat on the wooden chair near the fender looking into the fire. She was filled once again with a feeling of being the sole recipient of injustice. This feeling was not new, oh no. And she said to herself, If it isn't one thing with him, it's another. The last time, just before he went away, he had been on about 'Those are they'. She had been invited to tea with him and before she could eat a bite he had made her say twenty times 'Those are they' instead of 'Those are them'. It had happened because when he had asked her what she would like she had said, 'A squiggle.' 'A squiggle?' he had repeated. 'What are they?' And she had pointed to the thinly rolled slices of brown bread and butter and stated, 'Those are them.' So there had followed 'Those are they' twenty times. And then there was the day she had said 'was you'. She thought he had been going to have a fit that time. She had known well enough that it was 'were you', but when you didn't have time to think it just came out. Oh, she was fed up with grammar and everybody who talked grammar, so there! On this thought her mind was lifted to her two best friends, Beatrice Willoughby and Janice Schofield. They had lovely voices and talked ever so nice, and when she was with them she talked ever so nice too, and this afternoon, when she went to Beatrice's party, she would talk ever so nice. . . .

But who wanted to talk ever so nice on a farm? Her mind was suddenly brought from the uselessness of grammar on a farm to something Mr. Lord was saying. He was asking her mother what she knew about Lorna Johnson. Why was he wanting to know about Lorna Johnson? She looked towards him now and her mother, turning sharply to her, said, 'You can go out to play again, Mary Ann.'

She slid off the chair. She knew the technique. Her mother did not want her to hear what Mr. Lord was going to say about Lorna Johnson. But why should he want to talk about Lorna Johnson, anyway?

She was going through the scullery when she decided to wash her hands. The kitchen door was open, and if she were to hear anything while washing her hands, well, she couldn't help it. The kitchen door closed abruptly, and as she dried her hands she sighed.

She had just reached the back door when everything unpleasant was forgotten in a loud whoop of joy, for there was the lorry stacked high with timber turning into the farm-yard gate. Tony was at the wheel and next to him sat her da and their Michael. She raced down the path, along the road and into the yard, and greeted them all as they climbed down from the cab.

'Hullo, Da. You'll never guess who's back.' And before any of them had time to comment she went on, 'Mr. Lord, and he's in a tear.'

'He's back? But he wasn't expected until next week.' This comment came from Tony, and Mary Ann watched him and her da exchange quick glances. But they had no time to do anything more because Michael, speaking under his breath, said, 'Here he is now.'

They all turned and watched the old man approach them, and when he reached them his manner suggested that he had seen them all not longer ago than that morning, for he did not even stop to speak but addressed his grandson as he passed, 'The car's in Pellet's Lane; there's a puncture; see to it, will you, and then come up to the house.' His voice was quiet.

He was away out of the far gate and going up the hill towards his house before they looked at each other again, and then Mike, using the hook that replaced his lost hand, scratched at his thick, vigorous red hair and said under his breath, 'Well, that speaks for itself. What's happened now?' Slowly he turned his eyes down on his daughter. 'You been up to something again?'

Mary Ann blinked, her head bowed slightly, as she said in an offended tone, 'Well, I was only singin'.'

'Singin'?' Three pairs of eyes were levelled on her, and Mike repeated, 'Singin'? What were you singin' to put him in that mood?'

Mary Ann's head went lower. ' "He stands at the corner and whistles me out". I was just singing it to meself as I fed Penelope, and I was dancin' a bit, and then he barked at me from the gate.'

When the silence around her held, Mary Ann, looking up into the face of this beloved man, saw to her joy that his countenance was cracking. First his lids drooped and then his mouth moved from one side to the other. Then his big, straight nose twitched at the end, and to her immense delight he flung back his head and let out a bellow of a laugh that surely must have carried up the hill to Mr. Lord before he managed to stifle it.

Mary Ann, her face wreathed now in one wide grin, clapped her hands over her mouth, and when Michael asked, 'What song is that, Dad?' Mike said in mock surprise, 'You don't know "He stands at the corner"? Where've you lived all these years? Listen . . . it goes like this.' And placing his hooked hand on Michael's shoulder and his good arm around Mary Ann he walked them out of the yard singing under his breath, 'He stands at the corner and whistles me out, with his hands in his pockets and his shirt hanging out.' But when he came to 'Still I love him' he changed it to 'Still I love her', and the lift of his arm brought Mary Ann's feet from the ground and her laugh bubbling out again.

But before they reached the road Mike stopped and, looking round, seemed surprised not to see Tony following them. Tony was still standing looking in the direction his grandfather had taken, and Mike, calling to him, said, 'Come away in for a minute and have a drink of something.' And they stood waiting until he came up.

Tony, a young man of twenty-three, was, outwardly at least, a very good copy of his grandfather. He had the same leanness of body, the same thin features; he also, like Mr. Lord, carried his chin at an angle, and also, like his grandfather, he had a temper, but strangely he had shown very little of it in the last three years. His one concern seemed to be to please his grandfather, and, as Mike was not above saying, the old boy took advantage of this. Tony looked at Mike now and said in a voice which denied any connection with the Tyneside, 'I can't understand it. Why has he come back? I had a letter from him just this morning saying to expect him next Friday. There's something wrong somewhere; it just can't be her singing.' He looked down on Mary Ann now and smiled, and Mike said, 'You worry too much. I've told you afore, take him in your stride. He nearly had my hair white the first year I was here. I've got more sense now, and, anyway, he doesn't mean half he says. . . . Come on, come in and have a cup of something and listen to this, what she was singing, it's a grand ditty . . . edifying.' Mike laughed. Then, nodding his head slowly towards his daughter and raising his index finger, he beat time and counted, 'One, two, three', and on the word three she joined her voice to his and, grabbing his hand, went singing and swinging into the road and towards the house, with Michael and Tony coming up in the rear laughing.

'Well!' Lizzie exclaimed as she looked at her husband and daughter as they marched into the house still singing, and before she could voice any further opinion of the display, Mike, his deep and musical voice ringing out the words 'Still I love her', swung her around the kitchen floor.

'Stop it! Stop it this minute. Oh, Mike, don't be so daft, leave go.' When at last Lizzie had disentangled herself from Mike's arms she looked with disapproval on him and said sternly, 'It's all right you playing games and laughing, you should have been here a few minutes ago.'

'Well, all I can say is, if he was upset by a thing like that, then God help him. And don't look at me in that way, Liz, you can't lay it at my door. I never learned her that one.'

'Perhaps she learned it from . . . my friend Beatrice.' Michael was mimicking what he called Mary Ann's Sunday voice, and she turned on him in wrath, crying, 'Oh you! our Michael. Beatrice never learned me . . . taught me!' She bounced her head at him to emphasize her use of the correct grammar. 'Beatrice doesn't know songs like that.'

Michael, throwing his head back in a similar attitude to that used by his father, laughed, 'You're telling me . . . dear Beatrice is too dumb to know anything like that.'

'I'll smack your face if you call Beatrice . . .'

'That's enough! That's enough!' It was Lizzie speaking. 'Stop it, Michael. And you, Mary Ann, not so much of the smacking faces or we might finish up with the other end being smacked. And, anyway, who did you hear it from?'

In deep indignation Mary Ann looked at her mother, and in a voice and manner that once again spoke of the indignities of her life she said primly, 'Corny.'

'Corny?' Lizzie's eyes were screwed up in questioning perplexity when Mike put in, 'Don't be so dim, Liz. . . . Corny. You know Corny . . . Corny Boyle. That's who you mean, isn't it?' He turned and looked towards Mary Ann. 'Mrs. McBride's Corny.'

Lizzie's face was no longer screwed up but stretched wide now as she looked at her daughter and demanded, 'When did you see him?'

'When I was at Mrs. McBride's a week or so ago.'

Lizzie, continuing to look at Mary Ann, sighed deeply but said nothing. She remembered Corny Boyle and her memory made her shudder slightly. If ever a child went to the extreme to gather her friends it was her daughter. Corny Boyle on one hand and Beatrice Willoughby on the other. The poles were nearer than these two. She did not ask Mary Ann how long she spent in the company of Corny Boyle; she only had to use her imagination. Mary Ann had learned 'He stands at the corner' from him. But there was another matter Lizzie had to attend to at the moment, and its importance outweighed the doings of Mary Ann, and so she said to her, 'Go on upstairs now and get your things for this afternoon. I've ironed the ribbon to slot through your frock; leave the ends loose and I'll do the bow.'

Mary Ann looked hard at her mother for a moment. It was only eleven o'clock; she wasn't due at the party until four. As for slotting the ribbon through her frock, she wasn't going to put that one on; she was going to wear her nylon, her blue nylon. There was something up and her mother wanted rid of her.

She did not waste her still indignant glance on any other member of the family, but walked out of the room and up the stairs. And she was quick to notice that no voices reached her from the kitchen until she was across the landing, and then it was her mother's voice she heard and it brought Mary Ann to a stop. It also brought her head on one side and caused her ear to cock itself upwards, and what she heard her mother say was, 'You might as well know. It wasn't about her and the song that he was mad. He didn't like it, naturally, and he came in here and told me so, but it needs very little thought to realize that neither her nor the song had anything to do with him coming back unexpectedly like this.'

'You know what brought him?'

It was her father's voice, and now Mary Ann, retracing a number of her steps, was back at the head of the stairs when her mother's voice came again, saying, 'I've a good idea.' There followed a pause before Lizzie's voice, softer now and speaking to Tony, asked, 'Have you been going out with Lorna Johnson, Tony?'

Mary Ann's mouth dropped into a gape.

'Good God!' That was Tony saying that. He said it again. 'Good God! How could he know about that?'

'Aw, lad, don't tell me you've been so daft.' This was her father's voice, and it was unusually quiet and sort of sad, and Tony answered sharply, 'It was all so simple, it only happened the once. I was going into the cinema, there was a queue and I had to wait, and Lorna was standing not a yard from me. What could I do, pretend I didn't know her?'

'Did you come home together?'

'Yes.' Another pause. 'After we'd had supper. What was wrong in that? But it's as I thought, and I've had the idea

22

for a long time, he's been having me watched. . . . By damn! I won't stand for it. Oh no! I'm not standing for that.'

'Hold your hand a minute.' Her da's voice was lower still now. 'Don't jump to conclusions. He could have heard about it by accident.'

'What! In Naples?'

'Yes . . . well, you've got something there. But don't be rash. And I maintain what I said a minute ago. You were a fool to take her out, and to make it a supper an' all.'

'I couldn't get out of it, Mike; the situation was impossible. I see her every day.'

'You mean she sees you every day.' This was Michael speaking with unusual audacity, and he was promptly silenced by Mike saying, 'That's enough, quite enough.'

'Was it just that once, or are you seeing her again?'

Her da, Mary Ann realized, was talking as if he were Tony's da an' all, and when, after a short silence, Tony's voice came to her saying, 'Oh, what of it? I've made a date, but there's nothing in it,' her da said, 'You're mad.'

'All right, I may be, but I swear that if he keeps on I'll go the whole hog, I will. I've stood his iron hand for as long as I can, but this is a bit too much . . . spying on me, setting someone to spy on me. I'm going to have it out with him right away.'

She heard the scuffling of feet and her father's voice fading away, saying, 'Here, hold on a minute. Steady up. Let's talk this over.'

Her hand across her mouth, Mary Ann went softly into her room and closed the door. Tony had taken Lorna Johnson to the pictures, and not only to the pictures but out to supper. A cloud had passed over the sun. Tony had taken Lorna Johnson to the pictures. Tony was her property; he had always been hers. Always . . . all her life. Tony was her . . . her lad. He had said so himself, a long, long time ago.

She found that her face was twitching and she wanted to cry. But she mustn't cry, for her ma would want to know why. And then there was the party this afternoon. Bust the party; she didn't want to go to the party. Tony had taken Lorna Johnson to the pictures. She hated Tony . . . yes, she did. She hoped Mr. Lord would go for him. Oh no, she didn't, she didn't. She didn't want them to fight because Tony might lose his temper and go away. She could never hate Tony, but she hated Lorna Johnson. Oh yes, she hated Lorna Johnson. She hated all the Johnsons. Oh, she wished . . . she wished that they would die, all of them, especially Lorna. She went to the window and stood looking across the farm buildings in the direction of the two cottages, one of which was the home of the Johnsons.

A picture now filled the whole space of the farmyard. It was of a table. At one side sat Tony and at the other Lorna Johnson. She could see Lorna's high pencil-slim heels and short skirt. She could see her sheer nyloned knees. Her eyes travelled upwards over Lorna's close-fitting suit to her bold, dark eyes and black hair. She saw Tony looking at her across the table. Tony had that clean, washed look that was peculiar to him, and he was wearing his grey suit, the new one that he had bought last month and looked smart in. She saw him handing Lorna Johnson a plate, and on the plate were fish and chips. She watched Lorna nibbling at the fish and then . . . a wave of triumph passed through Mary Ann's slight body when she observed the smartly clad Lorna Johnson rolling on the unsubstantial ground in agony. . . . She had been poisoned and she would die and it served her right.

CHAPTER TWO

'GOOD AFTERNOON, MRS. WILLOUGHBY'

'Now mind your manners,' said Lizzie, as she buttoned the coat carefully over Mary Ann's blue nylon dress. 'Say "Good afternoon, Mrs. Willoughby", and when you are leaving don't forget to say "Thank you very much for having me, Mrs. Willoughby. I've enjoyed it so much". And don't forget to say "Mrs. Willoughby"; it's always nicer when you say the person's name. Do you hear?' She gave her daughter a slight shake.

'Yes . . yes, ma.'

'What's the matter with you? Don't you want to go to the party?'

'Yes . . . yes, ma.'

In some bewilderment Lizzie looked down on Mary Ann. Then, giving her a slight push, she said, 'Go on then, there's Tony waiting for you. And mind what I've told you and behave yourself.'

Mary Ann made no rejoinder to this. She walked sedately down the path, through the gate and on to the road where Tony was in the act of turning the car round. And when she was seated next to him she gave him no welcoming 'Hello' as was usual. Nor did he speak to her. He looked mad, in a temper. He had likely got it in the neck from Mr. Lord, and serve him right. Yet again she thought that it wasn't him she really wanted to get it in the neck, it was Lorna Johnson.

It wasn't until they were actually entering Newcastle that he spoke to her.

'What's the name of the street again you're going to?'

She turned to him and said coolly, 'It isn't a street, it's a drive . . . The Drive, Gosforth. Me ma told you. Number fifty-eight.' And then she added, in a further dignified effort to point out the difference between a street and a drive, 'It's a lovely drive, and a lovely house, beautiful, and they call it Walney Lodge. And Beatrice's father is a superintendent of ships, and her mother launches them.' She gave a little jerk to her head to add to this impressive statement, and for a flashing second Tony's eyes rested upon her, and there was a semblance of a smile on his face, but all the response she got out of him was, 'My! my!' and she didn't like the tone in which he said that.

When they finally reached Fifty-eight, The Drive, Mary Ann was quick to notice that while she was gushingly welcomed by her best friend Beatrice, Mrs. Willoughby and Tony were talking in the same kind of voices, high up in the head, sort of swanky. So it was with some bewilderment that Mary Ann received her hostess's welcome of 'Hullo, Mary Ann'. According to orders she answered, 'Good afternoon, Mrs. Willoughby', and in her best voice which, no matter how hard she tried, would not come out of the top of her head.

When she entered the hall hand in hand with Beatrice she recognized immediately the nice smell that had attacked her nostrils on her previous and first visit. It was a lovely smell and was all over the house. Not that – she now defended the smells of her own home – not that their house didn't smell nice, but theirs had a different smell, a bready smell, things-out-of-the-oven smell. This smell was scented, like flowers. Perhaps the smell was from flowers, for there, in front of the huge electric fire that Beatrice said burned imitation logs, there was heaped a wonderful array of flowers. They all sprang out of a low dish on the hearth. It was like a shallow baking bowl, not like the vases her ma put flowers in and stood on the window-sill.

She went up the beautiful staircase that had a wrought-iron balcony at the top through which you could look down into the hall below, but her mind was lifted from the beauty and unusualness of the house by her name being cried, and she turned round to see coming across the landing Janice Schofield, her other best friend.

'Oh, Mary Ann, isn't it lovely?'

Mary Ann did not know exactly to what Janice was referring, whether it was the house, or the party, or the meeting with herself after the long separation of a whole day, but she nodded brightly, and in the admiring and superior company of her two best friends she forgot for a moment about Tony and his cruel desertion. She was at the party and, oh, she was going to have a lovely time.

And Mary Ann did have a lovely time, for of all the fifteen guests she found herself prominently to the fore. Only one thing disappointed her: they did not have the television on. Between games and tea, and then more games and ice-cream, she glanced longingly towards the big white square eye of the world that stood on its pedestal in the corner of the large drawing-room. At one period towards the end of the wonderful party a fellow guest, a boy and another apparent television-yearning soul, suggested that they should switch on and see 'Bronco Layne'. Mary Ann seconded this by joining her hands under her chin and exclaiming, 'Yes! Oh yes!' but the young hostess squashed the plea immediately. Yet turned her refusal into a compliment by saying, 'Oh no, we don't want the silly television. You do one of your funny rhymes, Mary Ann.'

'What! Me?'

'Yes, go on.'

Mary Ann looked round now at the momentarily silent company and just for the smallest accountable fraction that one could measure in a second she felt shy. It was one thing to entertain her friends behind Sister Catherine's back and make them giggle by leaning towards them and whispering such things as 'Isn't it a pity that skitty Kitty can't be really witty.' This was considered excruciatingly funny because Sister Catherine's weakness was sarcasm. But it was quite another thing to . . . do some poetry . . . before a company.

'Do about the bluebottle,' cried Janice. 'Go on, Mary Ann, do about the bluebottle.'

'Yes, do.' Beatrice turned to where a smart young woman was leaning over the head of the couch watching the proceedings and cried, 'She makes them up, Aunt Connie. Oh, they're funny.'

'Come on, Mary Ann, do the bluebottle.'

So Mary Ann, standing with her back towards another arrangement of flowers that entirely covered the drawing-room fireplace, did the bluebottle. With a twinkle in her eye she began:

> 'He said it was a bluebottle,
> I said it was a fly.
> He said it was a bluebottle,
> And then I asked him why.
> Just 'cos, he said,
> Just 'cos that's all.
> Wasn't any answer,
> Was it,
> At all?'

The amusement came from the way Mary Ann delivered this more than from the words themselves, and there was much laughter and cries for more.

'Now do "The Spuggy".'

The slang term for a sparrow did not sound uncouth when coming from Beatrice's lips, but Mary Ann was apparently not quite happy at the suggestion she should do 'The Spuggy' – 'The Bloomin' Spuggy', to be correct. And, anyway, it wasn't one of her own. But the requests heaping on one another, she once again stood with her back to the flowers and began, in a north-country accent you could have cut with a knife, 'The Bloomin' Spuggy'.

> 'There was a bloomin' spuggy
> Went up a bloomin' spout,
> And then the bloomin' rain came doon
> And washed the bloomin' spuggy oot.
> Up came the bloomin' sun
> And dried up the bloomin' rain,
> And then the bloomin' spuggy
> Wentupthebloominspoutagain.'

This effort was greeted enthusiastically and with much laughter, especially by the young males of the party, and when Beatrice, basking in the limelight of her dear friend Mary Ann, cried, 'Now do . . .' she was abruptly cut off by her mother's polite tones, saying, 'No more, dear, now; the time's getting on. You've just time for one more game. Now what is it going to be?'

There were a lot of 'ahs' and 'ohs', and then it was decided the wonderful party would finish with hide-and-seek.

The choice seemed rather a young one for these ten-to-twelve-year-olds and Mrs. Willoughby raised her eyebrows to her cousin, the smart young woman, who was still leaning over the head of the couch.

Mary Ann, now very excited by her triumph, was determined to find some place to hide where she would never be found – well, not for a long time, anyway, she wanted this party to go on for ever. The majority of the guests were scampering on tiptoe through the hall and up the stairs, but Mary Ann made for the kitchen. It was a big kitchen; she had noticed this when she had helped to carry some of the plates from the dining-room. It was surrounded by tall cupboards, and one was a broom cupboard. It was the last cupboard, nearest to the back door. She knew this because she had seen Mrs. Willoughby opening it to get a cloth because somebody had spilt jelly on the floor.

The kitchen was empty and within seconds she had inserted her slight figure into a space between the standing and hanging brushes, and there she stood shivering with excitement, hoping and praying that this would be the last place that Beatrice, who was the seeker, would look for her.

When she heard the footsteps coming into the kitchen she bit on her lip and hunched her shoulders up over her neck. It was Mrs. Willoughby who had come into the kitchen and she was talking to Beatrice's Aunt Connie. She could hear the voices just as easily as if she was standing by their sides. Mrs. Willoughby was saying in her high, swanky voice, 'Hide-and-seek. It's a cover-up for Sardines, I suppose. Were we ever as goofy over boys as they are? I suppose we were, but it's really embarrassing to watch at times. Well, it's nearly over and thank goodness.'

'I don't know how you stand it, Jane. They've left the house in a frightful mess.'

'Oh, that will soon be cleared up, but I'll leave most of it until Mrs. Stace comes in in the morning. She's very good like that after a party, she doesn't mind coming in on the Sunday.'

'What did you think about . . . "The Spuggy"?'

'Oh yes.' There came a little laugh. 'I was dreading what she would follow up with.'

'She's a quaint little thing, isn't she?'

'My dear, Beatrice adores her.' There was another laugh. 'She's got a pash on her, as has Janice. I think it's because they're such opposites. You couldn't find two more opposite than Beatrice and her, now could you? . . . or Janice.'

'No, I suppose not, but she's rather taking, I think.'

'Oh yes, I grant you that, but there was a time when the sound of her name could make me scream. When she first came to the convent three years ago I got Mary Ann Shaughnessy for breakfast, dinner and tea.'

'What did you say her name was?'

'Shaughnessy.'

'Shaughnessy?'

'Yes. What's the matter?'

'Is her father a farmer, or a manager or some such?'

'Yes, he manages old Lord's farm. You know Peter Lord, the shipyard man. He's got a pet hobby of farming, I hear. But what's the matter, do you know them?'

Mary Ann, standing in her secret place, waited and the smart young woman's next words brought the thought to her mind that life could go on smoothly for months, even years, and then of a sudden everything happened together. Like today, Mr. Lord going for her, then finding out about Tony, and now the woman was saying in a low, pained tone, 'My dear, it's that child's mother that is the cause of Bob and me breaking up.'

'No, that's impossible. She must be just an ordinary woman.'

'Ordinary woman or not, she's the woman.'

'You must be dreaming, Connie.'

'I wish I were.'

'But I didn't know it was a woman that had caused the trouble. I thought it was . . . well . . .'

'Well, what?'

'Oh, I don't know – the growing pains of marriage, I suppose.'

'The growing pains of marriage don't usually cause separation, it's nearly always another woman, and in my case it's Elizabeth Shaughnessy.'

'But how do you know? Wait a minute until I close this door.'

Mary Ann, from within the darkness of the cupboard and the darkness that was now filling her small body, heard the footsteps go towards the kitchen door, and when they returned the smart young woman said, 'Just by chance, I suppose you would call it, or fate or some such . . . You remember when I went to open the sale-of-work 'in Shields last Christmas?'

'Yes, I remember.'

'Well, after it was over an awful old woman came up to me and made herself known. She said she had known Bob for years, and then she went on, with what she imagined to be deep subtlety, to tell me that she had nearly been Bob's mother-in-law. That for years he had courted her daughter but that in a moment of madness the girl had gone and married a big, red-headed good-for-nothing with the name of Shaughnessy, and she knew the marriage wouldn't last, as did Bob, and for a further number of years they apparently both hung on waiting for it to break up. And when it didn't and the man got this position as farm manager the old hag suggested to Bob that it was now time he stopped waiting. . . . In her own words, a man needs companionship and has to marry some time.'

'No, Connie !'

'Yes, my dear, it's a fact. I think I could have killed her. And guess how I felt when later Bob came to pick me up and in a few words verified all this woman had said, for he asked

31

most kindly after Elizabeth, most kindly. And that's putting it mildly.'

'Oh, but that was no proof. Now, don't be silly, Connie.'

'I'm not being silly; you don't know Bob as I do. You only see him as the charming, quiet individual. He had been morose and difficult for months, and I thought it was because I didn't want to start a family, but from that night I knew what the trouble was. He couldn't forget this woman.'

'Did you tackle him with it?'

'Yes . . . yes, I did. We had a few words about something, nothing to do with this. Then, as it goes, one thing led to another and I brought up this woman's name, this Elizabeth Shaughnessy. My dear, the guilt was written all over him; the very mention of her name made him jump as if he had been shot.'

'What did he say?'

'What do they all say? He denied it, of course. He didn't deny that he had at one time hoped to marry her, but he wanted me to believe that once she had married this fellow Shaughnessy all he wanted was her happiness. At the end, I asked him was he telling me that he hadn't hoped these two would split up and he bawled at me then and said, no, he wasn't telling me any such thing, and yes, he had hoped they would split up and he would have her, and that he would have her tomorrow if he could. And on that he packed his case and went.'

'Oh, Connie! It all sounds so silly. . . . And I know you, Connie. Ever since we were children you would keep on and on about a thing until the other person admitted you were right. Now you know you did.'

'I had no need to keep on about this, Jane. Anyway, the matter's finished. But it seems strange that that child should be this particular Elizabeth's daughter. . . .'

At this moment both the women jumped round with exclamations of fright and astonishment as the brush cupboard door was burst open and a tiny figure flew across the kitchen in the direction of the sink, and there, putting her head over the porcelain basin, vomited in no refined fashion.

Whereas Mary Ann just imagined that the three years she

had known Tony constituted the whole of her life, she had no need to bring her imagination into play when the name of Bob Quinton was mentioned, for one of her first memories was of hearing her Grannie speak his name and of the trouble that followed. It seemed to her that this man's name just had to be whispered and the harmony in her life was cut through as if by a sword's thrust. And she remembered the time when her mother had nearly left her da. If it hadn't been solely through Mr. Quinton, he, in the first place, had been the cause of the trouble, her da's trouble. Not even at the advanced age of twelve would she term it . . . drinking. Even though she no longer thought of him when in drink as just being sick, she nevertheless refused to look upon his lapses as getting drunk. .... Anyway, it was all because of this Bob Quinton that her da had had a number of lapses in the past.

She had prayed and prayed for years for something to happen to Mr. Quinton and God had got him married, which act had taken on the form of a miracle, but now the miracle had turned a somersault and they were back to the beginning. And this beginning was worse than the original one, for if Mr. Quinton could not like a smart, beautiful girl like Beatrice's aunt, then . . . then . . . It was at this point that her stomach had turned over and she had had to erupt herself from the brush cupboard.

The voices of Mrs. Willoughby and her cousin were passing back and forward over her head now. 'What a thing to happen. I wouldn't for the world have opened my mouth.'

'Well, how were we to know? It was this game they were playing. . . . But in the brush cupboard ! None of the others would have thought of going there. It's because she's so small. There, there, my dear, don't strain any more. Let me wipe your face.'

Mrs. Willoughby was taking a flannel gently round Mary Ann's face when the door burst open and Beatrice cried, 'Oh, here's Mary Ann.'

'Go away and close the door . . . do you hear me, Beatrice? It's time for things to finish now, anyway. Close the door, I say. Mary Ann's not well; she's having a bilious attack.'

The voices from the hall floated dimly to Mary Ann, saying, 'Poor Mary Ann.'

'Mary Ann's having a bilious attack.'

'Mary Ann's sick.'

'Poor Mary Ann.'

But their sympathy did not bring any easement to Mary Ann's tight breast.

'I'll get them into the drawing-room preparatory to packing them off, and then you can take her upstairs.'

When Mrs. Willoughby had hastily left the kitchen the young woman sat down and drew Mary Ann gently towards her knee, and then she said, 'Oh, my dear, what can I say?'

When Mary Ann made no response, she added, 'Did you hear everything?'

Mary Ann, her head cast down, gave it a small bounce and the young woman said, 'I – I didn't mean it, not all of it. Mr. Quinton and I have just had a little disagreement.'

Now Mary Ann's head came up and, looking straight into the smooth and beautiful face of Mrs. Quinton, she made a statement. 'My Grannie's a pig,' she said.

Mrs. Quinton's eyebrows gave a quick jerk and Mary Ann exclaimed again, 'She is. She's a pig. Me da used to say she was pig, hog, guts and artful, and she is.'

Mrs. Quinton's mouth was slightly open and her eyes were wide, but she could not find any words with which to answer this outburst, and Mary Ann went on, 'And me ma loves me da. Me da's a fine man. Everybody says so. Mr. Lord says so and he should know.' This latter was accompanied by a number of jerks from her head. 'And me ma thinks the world of me da, and she wouldn't leave him for anybody, not anybody.'

'I know she wouldn't, my dear. Don't upset yourself. There, there, please don't cry. Look at me.'

As Mary Ann looked into the deep brown eyes before her she was, in spite of her own grief, slightly surprised to see that they were blurred with tears, and again it was to her surprise when she found that this sight checked her own emotion and aroused in her a feeling . . . even a nice feeling . . . towards this person who had brought trouble back into her life, and she asked her now, very quietly, 'Do you like him?'

'Him? You mean Bo ... Mr. Quinton?'

Mary Ann nodded.

The lids were lowered, shutting the brown eyes away from Mary Ann's gaze for a second, and then they were opened wide again. And then Mary Ann got her answer. 'Yes, I like him, I like him very much, better than anyone else in the world.'

They looked at each other for a long time, then Mary Ann turned her head away and gazed at the floor. Her feelings at this moment, could she have transcribed them into words, would have been a profound reflection on the stupidity of men, men as a whole, but of Bob Quinton in particular. For Mary Ann's opinion was that Mrs. Quinton was nice, she was very nice, and lovely to look at, and Mr. Quinton must be mad to still want her ma. Not that her ma wasn't beautiful, there was no one more beautiful than her ma, but it was a different kind of beauty to that of Mrs. Quinton. So her profound thinking was summed up in three words: he was daft.

There came the sound of voices from outside the house, which suggested that the leave-takings were in progress. Some minutes later the kitchen door opened and Mrs. Willougby appeared, but she did not enter, she merely beckoned to her cousin and at the same time said gently to Mary Ann, 'Stay there a minute, my dear ... just a minute.'

It was a long minute. It stretched itself into five, and then ten. Mary Ann could hear voices in the hall outside the kitchen door. She knew they were those of Mrs. Willoughby and Mrs. Quinton. And once she thought she heard Tony's voice. Then she knew she hadn't been mistaken when the door opened at last and into the kitchen came Tony, accompanied by the two women. He looked gently at her for a moment before saying, 'Are you feeling better, Mary Ann?'

'Yes, thank you.' As she looked at Tony she knew he had learned all about Mr. Bob Quinton and her ma.

Her clothes were brought downstairs, and everybody helped to put them on her, and she was led from the house to the car like some sick personage. And into that particular section of her mind that was kept for such observations there slid the thought that you always got attention like this when you couldn't enjoy it.

It was only when she was seated in the car that she remembered that she hadn't thanked Mrs. Willoughby in the correct manner – in fact she hadn't thanked her at all. So, looking out of the window at her hostess, she said dismally, 'Thank you very much for having me, Mrs. Willoughby. I've had a lovely time.'

She was further surprised at the result of her good manners, for both Mrs. Willoughby and Mrs. Quinton bit on their lips and lowered their gaze from hers before turning away.

The car jerked forward and she was on her way home.

It was when the journey was more than half over that Tony stopped the car and, looking at her with his kindest glance, he said, 'You won't say anything at home about what you heard this afternoon, will you, Mary Ann?'

She stared at him blankly. What did he take her for? Did he think she was daft an' all?

Misinterpreting her silence, Tony added quickly, 'You know it would only cause trouble, and you know how fond your mother is of—'

'I know, I know.' Her chin was thrust upwards. 'I'm not going to say anything . . . I never say anything . . . I didn't afore.'

Tony's face was thoughtful as he looked down at this elfin, lovable, but unpredictable child. He still thought of her as a child. The tenseness of her face indicated to him just how she felt, but he guessed that her feelings concerning her parents' happiness wouldn't be those of a girl of twelve. Mary Ann's capacity for loving and hating was of an adult quality, and so it was with pain she suffered. He said no more, but smiled at her tenderly before starting the car again. . . .

'I told you to have bread and butter and not a lot of cake.' Lizzie looked sternly down on her daughter.

'There was no bread and butter, Ma. They don't have bread and butter, just sandwiches.'

'That's what you get for stuffing your kite.' Michael, seated at the table, was surveying her with a broad grin on his face, and she turned on him, but without vigour now, saying, 'I didn't stuff me kite, our Michael.'

'What made you sick then?'

She looked at her mother, and then at Tony, before turning towards her father where he stood with his back to the fireplace, and she said, 'It was likely the jumping and running about.'

'They were very pleased with her.' Tony spoke directly to Lizzie. 'They tell me she did quite a bit of entertaining.'

'Oh.'

The gaze of all her family was upon her now, and there was a touch of pride in Lizzie's voice as she asked, 'Did you recite . . . some of *Hiawatha*?'

'No, Ma.'

'Then what did you do?'

'I did the Bluebottle and I said—'

'Yes, what else did you say?'

Her answer was some time in coming, because she knew what reception it would invoke.

' "The Spuggy".' Her voice was very small.

'No! Mary Ann!' On Elizabeth's shocked tones there came a combined bellow from Mike and Michael, and Michael cried, 'She did "The Spuggy" before the Willoughbys! Oh, I wish I'd been there.'

Mike was now on his hunkers facing his daughter, his laughter rippling as he said, 'You should have gone one better, hinnie, and done "He stands at the corner". That would have shaken them, an' no mistake.'

'Yes, Da.' It was a quiet, dead response.

The laughter slid quickly from Mike's face. Michael's strident young bellow faded away. Elizabeth stood gazing down at her daughter. Then she watched her turn away from Mike and walk out of the kitchen towards the stairs.

Now Lizzie looked at Mike, and Mike looked at her and then towards Michael, and lastly they all looked at Tony. And Mike asked, 'Were they all right to her?' And Tony answered, 'More than all right, I should say. They were all very taken with her, saw her to the car, gave her the honours,

37

the lot.' He looked straight back into Mike's face as he spoke, and when Mike, although reassured, shook his head in perplexity, Lizzie said, 'Well, there's something wrong. She's not herself, and if I know her it isn't only a bilious attack.'

CHAPTER THREE

CORNY

THE situation called for prayer, not just a gabbled 'Our Father' and a 'Hail Mary'; nor being a participant at Mass. It needed a session to itself.

She had just sat through the Mass, but it hadn't left her with any feeling of comfort, so she had decided to wait behind until the church was clear and then go to the altar of the Holy Family. At one time she had been a frequent visitor at this altar. The troubles of her life had driven her to the steps of the Holy Family to beg, beseech and entreat them to make things better for her own family. And they had done so, though not without some little trouble on her own part. Nevertheless, her prayers had been answered. But Mary Ann, like the rest of humanity when things are going smoothly, forgot about the hard times, and the help she had received during them. So it was rather a shame-faced Mary Ann who now genuflected deeply to the altar of the Holy Family before kneeling and bowing her head. It must be said for her that she felt a little uneasy as she realized that although she had viewed them from the centre aisle week in week out for years she had never thought to come near them. And now when she was wanting something, here she was back again in the old position.

'Jesus, Mary and Joseph.'

She got no further. A long, long time ago when she had knelt here with her petitions she had thought that the Holy Family talked to her. Now she didn't imagine they were talking, but she knew without a doubt that their expressions were speaking louder than any words. The look on St.

Joseph's face said plainly, 'Well, what are you after now?' and Mary's expression, even in a gentle way, was saying, 'So you've come back?' and Jesus, who was not looking like a baby at all, His expression was saying the most, and it hurt the most, for it said, 'Even Sarah Flannagan would have come back and said thank you for all the good things that had happened to her.'

She bowed her head away from their reproachful glances wondering why Sarah Flannagan had to be brought into it. She couldn't pray to them, she couldn't ask them to do anything for her. After a long silence, during which she got a cramp in her legs, she fell back on St. Michael and the set prayer to him seemed to be quite in order with her own wishes.

'Blessed Michael the Archangel,
Defend us in the Day of Battle.
Be our safeguard against the wickedness and snares of the
 Devil.
Rebuke him, we humbly pray,
And do Thou, Prince of the Heavenly Host,
By the Power of God,
Send down to Hell Satan and all the wicked spirits
Who wander through the world for the ruination of souls.'

Ruination was her own word.

In the darkness behind her closed lids she saw St. Michael brandishing his sword, and falling under the brandishment ... was Mr. Quinton. And she was watching with satisfaction his quick descent into Hell, when she felt the tap on her shoulder. She gave a mighty start, followed by a gasp, as she opened her eyes to a white-surpliced figure standing at her side.

He was tall and grim-visaged, and not until he spoke did she realize that it was the head altar boy, who in actuality was no longer a boy.

'Father Owen wants to see you.'

She did not speak. She was still trembling from the shock of having imagined that the power of her prayer had called forth the saint.

She did not look at the Holy Family as she left their altar, but she was conscious of their eyes following her until she reached the vestry door and there saw Father Owen waiting for her. He was sitting on a wooden bench with one leg stretched stiffly out, and this he was rubbing vigorously. On the sight of her he stopped for a moment, saying 'Hullo, Mary Ann, come away in. I've got a touch of me rheumatics. It's the spring, I always get it in the spring. Sit down,' he added, then continued with his rubbing until the last altar boy had said good-bye to be answered with, 'Don't be late for Benediction, mind.'

The outer door closed, and, the vestry to themselves, the circular movement of Father Owen's hand came to a halt. Without any preamble he turned his head sharply to Mary Ann and said, 'Well, what's the trouble now?'

'Trouble, Father?' Mary Ann's eyes widened.

'Yes, I said trouble.' Father Owen's long head now drooped towards Mary Ann; and his eyeballs slowly disappearing backwards in his skull, he asked, 'What's wrong with your da?'

'Me da?' Mary Ann's whole face stretched with her amazement. 'Nothing's wrong with me da, Father; he's fine.'

Father Owen's head moved slowly to the front again and up, and his eyeballs returned to their natural position. 'Well, is your mother all right?'

'Yes, Father, me ma's fine an' all. We're all fine. And our Michael's going to sit for his G.C.E., and if he passes me da says he can stay on and later he'll go to college.'

Michael would have been astonished if he had heard with what pride she reported his progress.

'Yes, yes, Michael's doing fine. I know all about Michael. How is Mr. Lord? . . . Oh, but he's away.'

'No he's not, Father, he came back yesterday. He's all right an' all . . . but he's in a bit of a temper.'

Father Owen's head turned quickly again towards her as he asked, 'With you?'

'Just a little bit, Father.'

'What about?'

'Me grammar.'

The priest's head bobbed and he laughed now as he repeated, 'Me grammar.'

'My grammar, Father.'

'That's better. Well now, it would seem that you're all in very good health and spirits on the farm. . . . I forgot about Tony – how's he?'

'He's all right, Father.'

'Ah well, you've everything to thank God for, you're all all right.' The priest now turned himself completely round and, placing his palms on his knees with his elbows sticking outwards, he bent towards her and inquired softly, 'Well now, will you tell me, Mary Ann, why the Holy Family has had the honour of a visit from you?'

She stared back unblinking into the pale-blue eyes and she made no answer.

There was a quirk to the priest's lips now as he said, and still in a very soft voice, 'Would I be right in thinking that you went to enlist their assistance again in polishing somebody off?'

Mary Ann blinked once; it was a quick blink. All her life she had been under the impression that there was a close affinity between God and Father Owen, the only difference being that God was supposed to know everything whereas Father Owen actually did, at least concerning her.

'Were you praying for your grannie to die?'

She had her head down now. 'No, Father.'

That was the truth, anyway; she hadn't in those past few minutes when kneeling before the Holy Family asked them to polish off her grannie. But had her grannie come to mind when kneeling there the thought would have been accompanied, voluntarily or involuntarily, by the desire for her demise.

'Look at me, Mary Ann.' Father Owen's finger came under her chin and lifted her face towards him. 'Tell me, what's the trouble?'

'Nothing, Father.' Her lids were blinking rapidly now and the priest stared at her for a long moment before patting her cheek and saying, 'Ah well, come to confession Thursday night. Go along now and give my love to your mother and them all. Tell her I'll be running in to see her one of these days soon, and I'll want a big tea. Tell her that, mind.'

'Yes, Father, I'll tell her.' Mary Ann smiled. 'Good-bye, Father.'

'Good-bye, my child. Thursday night, mind.'

'Yes, Father.'

As Mary Ann walked up the aisle she knew for an absolute certainty now that there was not even a gossamer thread between God and Father Owen. No one but God himself would have realized that she couldn't talk about this matter in any other place but the confessional box. For years she had poured out her secrets to Father Owen in the confessional and they were safe with him. She could come out of the box and within a few minutes look the priest in the face knowing that all she had told him had been obliterated from his mind. It was as if he labelled her sins individually and sent them post haste to their different departments in heaven, there to be dealt with expertly. And once they were gone they were forgotten. . . .

Always during her short life when danger had threatened Mary Ann's loved ones she had sought the solution to her problems and solace for the hurt from three sources: the Holy Family, Father Owen, and lastly Mrs. McBride. The Holy Family were there to listen to her problems, Father Owen to give her advice about them, and Fanny McBride to bring an untranslatable feeling to her, untranslatable because it was a mixture of many things – easement, laughter, hope and pride. Oh yes, one main ingredient could definitely be picked out as pride, because in Fanny McBride her da had a great advocate. Fanny always made her feel proud of her da and today she wanted to feel extra proud of him, to hear that he was so wonderful that it was unthinkable even to suggest that anyone . . . anyone could take her ma from him. So now she did not make her way to the bus and home, but, ignoring the fact that she hadn't told her mother she was going to Mulhattan's Hall, and should her visit become known to Mr. Lord it would make him mad, she turned in that direction and walked towards Burton Street.

Although she hadn't lived in Burton Street for years, Mary

43

Ann was always instantly recaptured by the feeling of the place. Today it had the Sunday feeling, it was empty. Or almost. The front doors were closed and here and there a blind hadn't been drawn – those were the ones who didn't go to Mass, or chapel or church. The sight of these windows created in her a slight feeling of condemnation.

Before she reached Mulhattan's Hall she cast her eyes across the road in the direction of the Flannagans' freshly painted house, and her interest at this moment in the Flannagans was almost dormant. It was over a year since Sarah and she had met, and on that occasion they had passed each other without doing battle, for the simple reason that Sarah, being accompanied by . . . a lad, had refused to look at Mary Ann. Mary Ann did not wish to remember at this moment that the ignoring of herself by her enemy had cut her as deep as any slight and had been as provocative as an open challenge.

But now there was no sign of Sarah Flannagan, and this morning Burton Street was quiet. That was until she reached Mrs. McBride's window. Even before she came near it she knew that Mrs. McBride was . . . on; and when she had walked up the steps and across the fusty hall and knocked on her door, she had to repeat the knock twice before Fanny's strident voice yelled, 'Come away in then !'

'Hullo, Mrs. McBride.'

'Oh, hallo, hinnie. It's you. Come in, Mary Ann, come in. Come in and sit down. I'm just going at this one.'

This one was no other than Corny, Mrs. McBride's grandson and the only one of her many grandchildren for whom she had a strong liking. Corny was a tall boy of fifteen, a gangling, loose-limbed lad, with a face out of kindness one would call plain. It had one good feature: the shape of his mouth. Detached from its particular fixture Corny's mouth could have been termed beautiful, but in its present position its assets were outweighed by the other accompanying features. Again that was, until he smiled, or was deeply amused by something, and then his eyes, looking through his almost closed lids, held an infectious merriment that made the onlooker wonder about this gamin plainness. But at the present moment the plainness was very much in evidence, as was the look of frustration and irritation.

'Hello, Corny.' Mary Ann was pleased to see Corny.

'Hallo.' His voice was rough.

'Aw, you wouldn't open your mouth to him, Mary Ann, if you knew what he was up to. He makes me wild, he does.' Fanny was covering the distance between the oven and the table, and after banging on to the table a blackened meat dish holding a more than well done point-end of brisket, she cried, 'Look at that! Almost gone to a cinder, that's him.' She looked at Mary Ann while indicating her grandson with her thumb over her shoulder. 'You'll never guess what he's up to now, not in a month of Sundays you won't.'

'Aw, Gran.'

'Now shut your mouth, you; you've said enough already you have !'

Her fat body had turned swiftly towards her grandson, and now, turning as swiftly back again towards Mary Ann, she said, 'You know the trouble, lass, I've had with one and another, now don't you?' She did not wait for Mary Ann's reply but went on, 'It's all past so they say, all over and done with, but when my Jack married a Hallelujah, hell broke loose, and now, God in Heaven, you wouldn't credit it, not two in me own family, but this one here's goin' the same road.' Again she thumbed her grandson, and Corny broke in, 'Aw Gran, divint be daft. Aa'm not gannin the same road, it isn't the Salvation Army.'

'It's not a kick in the backside off it.' Fanny was now standing face to face addressing her grandson, and she brandished a long, black, double-pronged meat fork in her hand as she did so. 'What's the Church Army or Boys' Brigade, or somethin', but a first cousin to them ?'

'But, Gran, Aa'm not joinin' them.'

'No, not yet, but wait a week or so an' be God they'll have you in, as soon as you learn to blow that blasted cornet to their satisfaction. Then they'll have you in. Do you think they're goin' to learn you to play the thing as you said for nowt. Oh no, not if I know them Willies. If you had told me he was goin' to charge you a bob a lesson, then I would have thought nowt of it, but a bandmaster in the Boys' Brigade goin' to do something for nowt . . . Oh, away.' She flapped her hand at him, and he protested vehemently.

'Mr. Bradley's a nice man, he is, Gran. He doesn't want nowt off me, he just said Aa'd it in me to be a good player, if Aa'd some lessons. An' Aa only told you 'cos I thought you'd be pleased. . . .'

'Pleased – of course I'm pleased. You've made me Sunday.' Thrusting her arm right out, she pointed a podgy finger at him and, wagging it in front of his nose, she stated her ultimatum, 'I'm so damned pleased I'll tell you this. You go to that fella for lessons an' you don't come back here. And mind I'm tellin' you, you don't put your nose in this door. Now that's finished . . . ended, that's enough.' Fanny emphasized the end by showing her grandson the palms of her hands with her fingers spread wide, and he looked through them up into her face but said nothing. He just put his lips firmly together and moved his head from side to side and said nothing.

And now Fanny turned to Mary Ann and cried, 'Well now, sit down, me dear, and let's hear your crack. How's everybody up yonder?'

'Oh fine, Mrs. McBride.'

'Mike?'

'Oh, me da's grand.' And then Mary Ann added, 'I didn't tell me ma I was coming or else she would have sent you something, Mrs. McBride.'

'Oh, yer ma brought me a pile of stuff in last Wednesday, eggs, butter, the lot, and a chicken the week afore. Your ma keeps me supplied . . . Lizzie's a good friend.'

Mary Ann looked at Mrs. McBride and her mouth dropped open to repeat, 'Me ma here last Wednesday?' Her ma hadn't said she came to Mrs. McBride's every week. A soft understanding smile spread over Mary Ann's face. Her ma didn't want her to come too often to Mrs. McBride in case it upset Mr. Lord, but she was seeing to it that Mrs. McBride didn't go short of titbits. Her ma was nice; oh, her ma was nice.

'Will you have a bit dip and bread. Look, it's nice fat.' Fanny indicated the grease in which the brisket was swimming, and Mary Ann, looking towards the fat, felt her stomach give a little heave. But she managed to smile as she said, 'No, thank you, Mrs. McBride; it would put me off me dinner and then me ma will go for me.'

'Aye, perhaps you're right. What about you?' Her countenance was disgruntled as she addressed her grandson, and the substance of Corny's answer was the same as Mary Ann's. 'Aa'm not hungry,' he said.

'That's a change; something's going to happen. My God, you not hungry . . . world catastrophe imminent.'

On this statement they all, after a second's hesitation, simultaneously burst out laughing, and Fanny sat down, crying, 'Oh, I'm not the woman I was. I can't laugh as long or as loud. I have no puff now.'

Mrs. McBride had been very ill; they had thought she was going to die. But Mary Ann couldn't see her friend dying. Mrs. McBride was Mrs. McBride and would go on forever.

Mary Ann regaled her now with her own particular news of the farm and listened yet once again to Mrs. McBride telling her she had always known that Mike had it in him to be a grand farmer. The conversation was most satisfying, and when half an hour later she went to take her leave she was not displeased that Corny, who had been mute since his battle with his grannie, now made it evident, and without words, that he, too, was about to take his leave. And this called forth comment from Fanny.

'You not stayin' for your dinner?'

'No, Gran; me ma wants me across home.'

'You didn't say that afore.'

'Ya didn't give me a chance, Gran.'

'Have you got somethin' special?'

'No, nowt that I know of.'

'Well, why do you want to go skiting off?' Whether it was an unusual thought had struck Fanny or whether she was checked by the expressive hunch of her grandson's shoulders, she stopped her cross-questioning and, looking at Mary Ann, she smiled broadly, saying now, 'All right, get yersels along and my love to your ma and da, hinnie.'

'Bye-bye, Mrs. McBride.'

'Bye-bye, hinnie. And thanks for comin'; it does me good to see you. . . . So long, you.' She accompanied this last terse farewell with a dig from her thick fist in her grandson's back, and he, bestowing on her now an affectionate grin, replied, 'So long, Gran; be seein' ya.'

'Aye, be seein' ya.'

She led them out of the door and watched them walk side by side down the steps. 'So long,' she called again. And they answered her, 'So long.'

As Mary Ann walked down the street with Corny she began to experience an odd sensation. She was pleased to be with Corny . . . yet she was ashamed, and she was ashamed of being ashamed. It was rather confusing.

She glanced sideways at him . . . up at him, for he was almost twice her height. His clothes looked funny, not a bit like the boys' who were at Beatrice's party. Both the ends of his trouser legs and the cuffs of his jacket seemed to be moving farther and farther from their appointed places with each step he took. She realized that he had outgrown his suit, and she felt slightly indignant that his mother hadn't done something about it.

He now turned and, catching her eye on him, he smiled as he said, 'Me grannie's a tartar, isn't she?'

'She's nice.'

'Aye, she's aal reet is me grannie. Aa divint knaa what Aa'd dee if Aa hadn't her.'

This seemed an unusual remark for Corny to make, at least Mary Ann thought so. If three weeks ago, before their first meeting for some long time, she had given a thought to Corny Boyle her mental picture would have presented her with a dirty-nosed, dirty-faced teasing lump of a lad, of whom, had she been truthful with herself, she was afraid, but these two brief meetings had shown her a different Corny altogether. She was at this moment wishing that she hadn't to take the bus and he could walk all the way home with her, yet at the same time there was this feeling of being ashamed to be seen with him in such clothes. And, moreover, she was finding that she was criticizing his way of speaking. Mrs. McBride talked broad and she liked to hear her, and she herself could talk a bit broad, but now, alone with Corny, she had an urge to talk proper, even to talk out of the top of her head like Beatrice. She also became more confused by her feelings when she realized why she wanted to do this ... it was in the hope that he would try to copy her ... and talk, well, if not proper, a bit different from what he did.

The hope was strangled even as it struggled for birth by the sound of Corny's voice saying in his rich Geordie accent, 'Hev ya heard Eddie Calvert?'

'Heard Eddie Calvert?' Her words were precise. 'Who is he?' Even to herself she didn't sound like herself.

'He's a cornet player. Why ... the best. By lad, he can myek her taalk. Mr. Bradley says if Aa stuck at it Aa could myek a go of it an' be as good as him ... Eddie Calvert. ... But there' – the gangling limbs seemed to fold up at this point – 'Aa've got neewhere to play. Neebody wants to hear yer practisin' the cornet.'

Mary Ann forgot for the moment about talking properly, she forgot about being ashamed of his suit or the broadness of his twang; she seemed to forget everything, even the revelations by Mrs. Quinton yesterday, the revelations that could shatter the harmony of her home. Everything at this moment was forgotten but the desire to comfort and please Corny. The sudden shyness that was accompanying this desire forced her to look straight ahead as she said, and in her ordinary voice now, 'I like hearing you practising. You playcd nice that morning. And me da knows the song you were playing. If you want to practise there's plenty of space on our farm, and me da wouldn't mind you comin', I know he wouldn't. ... Nor me ma.' She ignored a pause in her thinking at this point which seemed to check her tongue, and went on in a gabble now and looking at him as she walked. 'It's my birthday on June the first. You can come to me party – that's on the Saturday – if you like, and you can play ...'

He had stopped and was looking at her, his face straight and his voice unusually quiet now as he said, 'Yu mean that? Yu're not just kiddin'?'

'No. No, I'm not. Yes, I mean it.'

And she did mean it. Every fibre of her meant it. As she

looked into his now gently smiling face, she meant it. As they turned and walked silently now towards the bus stop, she meant it. As he stood looking at her through the window of the bus, she meant it. She meant it more than ever as she went along the road towards the farm. She meant it until she looked up the hill towards Mr. Lord's house, and then she stopped, and with her gaze fixed on the imposing structure she said defiantly, 'Well, it's just his suit.' Yet before she reached home she knew it wasn't just Corny's suit; and as she entered the house she could see Mr. Lord and Corny confronting each other and she exclaimed to herself, 'He'll have a fit.'

And there was no need to explain to whom she referred.

CHAPTER FOUR

MIKE PASSES HIMSELF

MONDAY morning, as is generally understood, sets the main pattern for the week, and the scene in the kitchen before Mary Ann departed for school indicated a stormy time ahead.

In bed last night Mary Ann had realized that if she had told her ma of the extended invitation to Corny immediately on entering the house it would have been over and done with, but she hadn't, and so following a night of weird dreams dominated by Corny, dressed in a smaller suit still, blowing his cornet into Mr. Lord's face, she decided she must tell her ma before she went to school. Strategically she left the telling until almost the last minute. And now the place was in an uproar.

'Whatever possessed you, Mary Ann? After asking Beatrice and Janice and the rest!'

'Not forgetting Roy Connor.' This last remark was an almost unintelligible exclamation from Michael.

Roy Connor, the product of a private school, had last year entered the grammar school and was, in Michael's estimation, a pie-eyed cissy.

Mary Ann could give no attention to her brother, for her whole mind was on her mother and the temper she was in. Even her da was not coming to her assistance; he was apparently indifferent to the situation and was standing filling his pipe as if nothing was happening.

But here Mary Ann was wrong, for following Lizzie's next remark Mike joined the fray.

'You'll just have to tell him you can only have a certain

number and you've already asked them. . . . Anyway, I don't care what you tell him, the boy cannot come. You've got yourself into—'

'Hold your hand a minute, Liz; hold your hand a minute.' Mike closed the lid of his tobacco tin and placed it in his pocket before adding, 'She's asked him. The thing's done, and she can't back out of it now.'

'You keep out of this, Mike. . . . Have you seen Corny Boyle in this last year or two?'

'No, I haven't, but I remember the lad.'

'Well' – Lizzie drew herself up – 'that should be a reference for an invitation to her party.'

'She says he's changed.' A jerk of his head indicated Mary Ann. 'He must have, for as I remember, she was scared of him.'

'Yes, he's changed all right and not for the better . . . at least in looks. You should see him and the way he's turned out.'

'Well, that's likely his mother's fault. Anyway, she can't get out of it now.'

'Do you know what the result would be if he came down?' A jerk of Lizzie's head indicated the house on the hill and its master, and on this Mike turned swiftly and said angrily, 'If he comes he's welcome, and if he doesn't like the people in the house, then he knows what to do. Corny Boyle's been asked and Corny Boyle's coming and that's that.'

Mary Ann watched her da stalk out of the room; and watched her mother put her hand to her throat and close her eyes; she watched their Michael draw in his lips and shake his head at her, and she wished she was dead.

'Don't you ever think, child?' Lizzie was looking at her with reproach-laden eyes.

'He had nowhere to play his cornet and . . .'

'Oh, my God!' Lizzie now put her hand over her eyes. It was very rarely she used such an expression, and it indicated to Mary Ann the depth of her feelings on this matter.

'He's not playing that cornet here. I'll throw the thing in the pond.'

Mary Ann turned her glance on Michael now. Under

other circumstances her retort would have been, 'You try it on and it'll be you who'll land in the pond.' Although there was a year's difference between Corny and Michael, Corny could already give inches to her brother. But she held her peace. Michael, being another boy, could make it tougher for Corny than her mother could . . . that's if he ever reached the party.

'Go on.' Lizzie's voice had a low, hopeless note now. 'You'll miss your bus; we'll sort this out later.'

'Bye-bye, Ma.' Mary Ann's voice, too, sounded hopeless.

'Bye-bye.'

It seemed an effort for Lizzie to stoop and kiss her daughter, and Mary Ann left the house with the weight of the world on her shoulders. But as she passed the farm gates her da came from behind the open byre and, looking down on her, he said quietly, 'Don't worry, everything will be all right. Corny'll come. Go on now.' And again he repeated, 'Don't worry.'

So the week began.

On the Monday afternoon Sister Catherine gave Mary Ann a hundred lines for not paying attention. It was odd that she had 'not paid attention a hundred times before'. She had entertained her friends at the sister's expense, she had done a number of things for which she could have been given lines, but today, because she had done nothing, and literally that, she got a hundred lines. It was all so unfair.

On the way home she lost her bus pass. Added to this, a very strained welcome from Lizzie when she reached home completed the Monday.

On Tuesday, on her return from school, she heard that there had been trouble on the farm with the new bull whose name was Neptune. He had kicked out at Len when he was being groomed; and Len said his rightful place was at the bottom of the sea, and if he had his own way . . . etc.

Mary Ann was not surprised to hear Neptune had kicked out; she didn't like Neptune and never went near him. Great William, the old bull, was her favourite. He was known as Bill and would let you rub his nose.

Also on this Tuesday she learned that Mr. Lord and Tony

had been at it, because Tony, she understood, would not cancel his date with Lorna Johnson. Tony, to her mind now, deserved everything he had evidently got from Mr. Lord. She saw no similar situation in the fact that she could not cancel her invitation to Corny.

But Monday and Tuesday were nothing to Wednesday. The trouble on Wednesday started early with the arrival of the postman. Before Lizzie opened the letter everyone knew who it was from; and when with her breakfast half finished she read it, then laid it by the side of her plate without making any comment, the silence at the table was a waiting silence. It wasn't until the meal was finished that Lizzie, with the air of making a casual remark, said, 'My mother's looking in on Saturday.'

Oh no! The protest was loud inside Mary Ann's head. Saturday, the only day she hadn't to go to school, the only day she could romp on the farm from early morning till late evening, and her grannie had to come on Saturday. That her grannie had to come at any time was something in the shape of a catastrophe, but on a Saturday!

It wasn't until Mike was putting his coat on preparatory to leaving the house that he made his remark, also in a casual tone, 'I'll change me day off,' he said. 'I've got things to do in Newcastle; I'll make it Saturday.'

'Oh, Mike!' Lizzie sounded hurt, all pretence gone now. 'You know she'll hang on and hang on waiting for you to come in.'

'She won't unless she stays the night, and she'll not stay the night under my roof, you know that, Liz.'

'It'll only make things worse.'

'Now look here, Liz.' Mike turned and confronted his wife. 'It's months since she was here, I know, and months before that when she paid us a visit, but does she ever change? That woman's got the devil in her and she'll never let up on me until I'm dead, and not even then. I know her, Liz, I know her. The only thing I don't know and don't understand is how she comes to be your mother.'

'Oh, Mike!'

'It's no good, Liz. I'm takin' me day off on Saturday.

Perhaps I'll take me daughter into Newcastle with me, eh?'
He put his head on one side and caught Mary Ann's glance,
and brought from her the only joyful note of the week so far,
'Oh yes, Da; that would be lovely.'

And this is how Mike and Mary Ann happened to be in
Newcastle on a Saturday morning and, of all places, in
Durrant's.

Mike had done his business at the bank, he had been to the
corn-chandler's, he had been to the garage about spare parts
for the tractor, he had been to an office and talked with a
man about the show in Castle Douglas, and then he had said,
'What about a drink?'

It was at this point that they were passing Durrant's. Mary
Ann had heard of Durrant's. Beatrice and her mother some-
times went there, as did Janice and her mother, and so with
daring she put her suggestion saying, 'Da, Durrant's is nice;
you can get coffee and cakes there.'

Coffee and cakes, she knew, held no attraction for Mike,
who by this time of the morning and on his one visit a week
to Newcastle would have a thirst for a drink . . . a real drink,
but a limited drink. For three years now he had never broken
his solemn vow not to go over two pints and a double. This
treat, only once a week might for him be near the line of total
abstinence, yet it was enough to make him feel that he could
still take it if he wanted it. Although he knew he should never
go beyond this line, for his own self-respect he did not look
upon it as a compulsory line.

Mike now, looking down on Mary Ann with a deep twinkle
in his eye, repeated, 'Coffee and cakes in Durrant's? And
why not? We've been let out.' He squeezed her hand and
then, with a lift to his broad shoulders and a tilt to his head,
he pushed his daughter before him and entered Durrant's.

There were big tables and small tables and people dotted
all round, and Mary Ann's proud gaze swept over them, and
in its sweeping it was checked and brought back to a near
point and focused on a high white, gauze-trimmed hat, and
beneath it two large brown eyes that were looking at her.
The owner of the hat was not a couple of arm's lengths away
from her and, smiling, she said, 'Hullo, Mary Ann.'

Mary Ann had stopped, causing Mike to stop behind her, and now she cast a swift glance upwards at her da before looking again towards Mrs. Quinton.

'The lady's speaking to you, Mary Ann.'

'Hullo.'

'I'm waiting for Beatrice.' After making this statement Mrs. Quinton's eyes lifted from Mary Ann to the big red-headed man standing at her side and she said, 'You're Mary Ann's father?'

'Yes. Yes, I'm Mary Ann's father.' The two adults smiled at each other.

'Are you looking for a table? Won't you sit down here? Beatrice will be delighted to see you.' Mrs. Quinton addressed the latter part of her remark to Mary Ann, and Mary Ann, looking once again up at her da, waited.

'Thanks. Come along, sit down.' It seemed that Mike had to press Mary Ann into the seat before he took his own opposite Mrs. Quinton.

'Mary Ann hasn't introduced us but I'm Mrs. Quinton.'

'Mrs. Quinton!' Mike's voice showed pleased surprise. 'Well, well.'

'You know my husband, of course?'

'Yes . . . yes, I know your husband. Yes, I know Bob.'

Mary Ann could gather nothing from her father's remark. What she did gather was that he seemed quite at ease in this posh café and quite at ease talking to Mrs. Quinton, and she was posh an' all. And she noticed something else: Mrs. Quinton kept her eyes fixed on her da as if she found him nice. Slowly the tension began to seep out of her body. In some inexplicable way she felt that this meeting did not worsen the situation, and that the menace of Mr. Quinton was in some way lessened by it.

'How is Bob? I haven't seen him in years.'

'Oh.' The brown eyes were hidden for a moment by a flickering of lids, and then Mrs. Quinton said brightly, 'Oh, he's very well . . . very well.'

Mary Ann noticed that her da made no further remark on the subject of Mr. Quinton's health but that he kept his eyes on Mrs. Quinton and asked, 'What's he doing now?'

'Oh, building ... building as usual.'

'Anything in particular?'

'Well ... er ... he's doing some houses up Low Fell way. ... Did you hear about the party on Saturday?' Mrs. Quinton, jumping from one subject to another, now looked at Mary Ann and there was a question in her eyes, but it wasn't answered by Mary Ann, for Mike replied, 'I hear you gave her a grand time.'

'Yes, yes. ... Ah, here's the waitress.'

'Let me see to it.'

Mrs. Quinton made no protest and Mary Ann listened to her da giving the order for coffee for four. He did it as if he came to Durrant's every day and ordered coffee; and when he turned again to Mrs. Quinton and began to talk, Mary Ann sat looking at him, her mouth slightly agape. He never talked like this to her ma, nor had she heard him talk like this to anybody else. Not that he was putting it on, but he was talking nice and ... passing himself. If she didn't know he was her da she would have taken him for a man like Mr. Willoughby, a gentleman, or her own Mr. Lord, who never dirtied his hands and always wore a blue suit and collar and tie. She had seen her da in all kinds of moods, drunk and sober. She had, to her deep shame, seen him singing in the street when he was as full as a gun. She had seen him crying with shame. She had seen him standing up to Mr. Lord. But never before had she seen him entertaining a lady to coffee. It was a revelation to her, a joyful revelation. Oh, she was so proud ... her da could pass himself.

It was more than twenty minutes before Beatrice put in an appearance and she gushed over Mary Ann, and Mary Ann, relieved for the moment of all worry and responsibility and basking in the gentlemanly glory of her father, returned Beatrice's effusion, and over yet another cup of coffee and some more cake Mary Ann let herself go and jabbered to her friend and forgot to feel responsible for her da.

It was fifteen minutes later when they all parted company and Mary Ann watched her da shaking Mrs. Quinton by the hand and saying, 'Now remember me to Bob. And don't forget what I told you: you look us up. We're always at home, and Lizzie would be delighted to see you.'

Mrs. Quinton assured him that she would do as he asked, and added to this the unnecessary remark that she hoped they would meet again.

'You didn't tell us that you had met Mrs. Quinton at the party.'

Mike was striding along looking ahead as he spoke, and Mary Ann, after a moment's pause, said, 'I forgot, Da.'

'Did you see Mr. Quinton on Saturday?'

'No, Da.'

There was a break in the conversation as they became divided by a trio of prams, and when they came together again Mike went on, but more so now as if he were asking himself a question and not her: 'Why did she say he was on houses up Low Fell? They were finished more than a month gone. I passed through there over three weeks ago and the place was all tidied up.'

Mary Ann now put in quickly, 'We mustn't forget me ma wants that ribbon binding for the blankets, Da.'

Mike looked at his daughter for a moment and then he laughed. She couldn't make out why he was laughing, but when he grabbed her hand and pulled her to him she did not search to know. The tone of the day was set.

They did more shopping. Then Mary Ann waited while Mike went in and had his drink. She did not have to wait long, for he seemed to be in and out in no time. Then around one o'clock they had a good dinner. And afterwards went to the pictures.

It was a glorious day, and when towards evening they made their way home in the bus Mary Ann was bursting with the events of it. So many things had happened, nice things, but the crowning one was that her da had passed himself. He had talked to Mrs. Quinton, and Mrs. Quinton had liked him talking to her.

As always when filled with joy she wanted to hitch and skip, to throw off her exuberance, and she started, as soon as they left the bus, by hitching along the grass verge. It wasn't until they reached the farm gate that she stopped, as Mike, with a critical eye on her, remarked, 'We're in for a dampener if she hasn't left yet.'

Oh . . . her grannie! She hadn't thought about coming home and finding her grannie. It certainly would put the tin hat on everything if her grannie was still in the house.

Being of the same mind and not wanting to confirm their suspicions, they did not go straight to the farm-house. Mike, turning into the yard, went towards the office, there to deposit some samples he had with him. Mary Ann, still bubbling with excitement, skipped towards the cow byre just to have a . . . peep in, until her da made his appearance again.

But between Mike's office and the cowshed was the bull-pen, Bill's bull-pen. The pen had two doors, one leading into the open section and one into a covered part that had at one time been a small byre but which had been given over to make a very comfortable house for Bill. Bill had his own doorless aperture which led from the byre into his private yard. The gate leading from the open section into the farm-yard proper had a slip catch which could only be opened from the outside, as also had the door leading into the byre part. Mary Ann had been warned never to lift the latch of the open pen gate, but this warning was not extended to the byre door because even when the byre door was open there was a barricade about a yard's distance from the door. This was the back structure of what had at one time been the feeding bins and had been left as an added security against the bull getting out. It had an opening at the end big enough for a man to enter but not big enough for the bull to come through.

Mary Ann, after lifting the wooden latch from the door, entered the byre and, looking over the partition into the dim region beyond, she said, 'Hullo there, Billy Boy. . . . Come on, scratchy noses.' When this soft endearment was answered by a low rumbling roar she laughed and said, 'You in a bad temper, Bill? Come on, and I'll scratch your nose.'

Apparently Bill was in a bad temper, for he pawed at the straw under his feet and again emitted a dull roar.

As she was once again about to tempt him with endear-

59

ments a voice from behind her in the yard said, 'Oh, hullo there, what you up to?'

She turned her head to take in at a glance the, to her mind, under-dressed figure of Lorna Johnson, and she answered briefly, 'I'm talking to Bill.'

'No accounting for tastes.' Lorna had taken a step nearer and was now standing in the doorway of the byre.

'Come on, Bill, come on.' Mary Ann, her voice low and wheedling, was still persisting with her coaxing, and as she did so she wondered what had got into Bill and at the same time what Lorna Johnson was doing in the farmyard because it was no secret that Lorna didn't like animals; she was even afraid of cows.

In the next moment Lorna made it clear why she was in the yard, for taking a wary step to Mary Ann's side she said in a lowered tone, 'Have you seen Tony about?'

Mary Ann's eyes flickered sharply upwards to the heavily made-up face, and her tone was flat and curt as she answered, 'No, I haven't.'

Lorna gazed steadily down on Mary Ann and then, with a twisted smile breaking the painted moulding of her lips, she said, 'And you wouldn't tell me if you had, would you?'

'No, I wouldn't.'

'No, I thought you wouldn't . . . you're a blasted little cat.'

Mary Ann's face widened with indignation. She did not like Lorna Johnson, she had never questioned Lorna Johnson's feelings towards her, but now she knew them without any doubt. Then Lorna Johnson said something that Mary Ann could not quite take in. She said, 'Well, my little madam, your days are running out, and if I can do anything about it I'll help them along, you damned little upstart, you.'

All this was delivered in a low tone. The tone even suggested that Lorna could have been saying something quite pleasant, and although Mary Ann could only half understand the implication of the words she realized full well that they were derogatory and she was mad at Lorna Johnson, and she knew that if she didn't get away from her she would cheek her, with the result that she would get walloped. So without more ado she swung away from the girl and, leaving the byre, pushed the door closed after her. This action was merely an off-shoot of her anger combined with the habit of always closing the door when coming out of the byre. It had no premeditation whatever about it. It did cross her mind at this moment that she was leaving Lorna Johnson in there with the bull, and Lorna was afraid of the animal. But she had taken no more than three steps from the byre door when a combination of sounds turned her about so swiftly that she almost leapt from the ground.

She could not tell which she heard first, whether it was the heavy wooden latch dropping into the slot as the door banged, or the ear-piercing screech of Lorna, or the terrible bellow of the bull, but in the next instant she found herself frantically trying to unlatch the door. At other times it had always been quite easy. Though the slot where the wooden latch fell into was deep, the sides were smooth and lifting the latch was a simple matter of a second, or it had been until this moment. Whether the latch had actually stuck or it was the terrifying sound of Lorna and the bull apparently trying to out-yell each other, Mary Ann found that she couldn't get the latch out of its socket.

Then, on the point of screaming herself, she felt her body lifted from the ground, and as she hung dangling from a great hand she saw the latch being swung up and the door pulled open. And as her feet touched the ground again she saw Lorna staggering into the yard, her mouth wide and the screams still issuing from it.

'It's all right, it's all right. There, you're all right.' It was Mr. Johnson's voice shouting above his daughter.

'Sh . . . sh . . . she lo . . . locked me in. Sh . . . sh . . . she . . . lo . . . lo . . . locked . . .'

'All right, you're all right. . . . She did, did she? You . . . you blasted little swine !'

It was Mary Ann who now screamed. She screamed as Mr. Johnson's hands gripped her shoulders. Then for the next second or so she did not know where she was, she only knew she was being shaken and thought her head would fly off at any minute. She was gasping and choking so much that she couldn't get her yells out. And then she felt as if she was being pulled in two. Her feet touched the ground and she fell on to her bottom with a plop. Before her bouncing vision she now saw her da facing Mr. Johnson.

She saw her da's fist go out and Mr. Johnson's arms flaying, then Mr. Johnson fell down, and as he hit the ground he gave an awful cry. It was this last cry, with its high screeching quality, that outdid both Lorna's and her own screams and the bull's roaring and caused a blackness to surround Mary Ann. Although she could see nothing she could still hear voices, and before she fainted away she was aware that the yard was full of voices, among them her mother's and Tony's. . . .

She rose struggling out of the thick blackness to find herself on the couch in the kitchen, with her mother bending over her, saying, 'Drink this.' But she couldn't make herself drink. As her da was wont to say when he was very tired, 'I haven't got the list to lift a hand,' so she felt now. She could scarcely lift her eyelids to look at her mother, but even the little she saw of her was enough to convey dimly to her that her mother was vexed, even angry, and she had the feeling for a moment that she wanted to pass out again, to escape from the look. But the sensation of fainting was still so near to her that she rejected this idea and lay still. With the passing moments she became more aware of what was taking place about her, and when her mother said again, 'Drink this', she drank from the cup, then lay back and closed her eyes.

She was aware from time to time of her mother and Michael and Tony whispering, but she was too tired to make an attempt to listen. That was, until she heard Mr. Lord speaking. She didn't know if his voice was coming from the far end of the kitchen or outside the house, but she heard him say plainly, 'Nice state of affairs, Shaughnessy. The man's ankle is broken as clean as if you had cut it with an axe.'

'Should have been his neck.'

'Well, he has his own opinion on that. He tells me you struck him first.'

'Who's denying it? He was shaking her like a rat.'

'It's understandable when you give it a little thought. The man was upset about his daughter. I myself would not like to have been locked in that place with Neptune.'

Neptune? It was William. Or was it? Faintly she remembered the unusual roar of William. Eeh! It couldn't have been Neptune. She herself would never go near Neptune. . . . And then another thought, weak yet gathering strength of conviction: she hadn't locked her in . . . she hadn't locked Lorna Johnson in, that was a lie.

Then Mr. Lord's voice came again, 'There will be an outcome of this business; that man'll make trouble.'

'Let him.'

'What are you going to do for someone in his place?'

'I'll manage.'

A few minutes later she felt forced to open her eyes, and there above her she saw the thin, wrinkled face of Mr. Lord, and in an odd intuitive way she realized that for all his stiffness and the sound of his voice he wasn't mad about the business, not really mad. But her da was mad, as was her ma.

'Are you feeling better?'

'Yes.'

'Do you think you're able to talk?'

'Yes.'

'What induced you to lock that girl in the bull-pen?'

'I didn't.' She would have liked to take her denial further but she hadn't . . . got the list.

'They say you did.'

'I pushed the door as I was going out . . . the latch must have dropped . . . it was stuck.'

'Why was that girl in the bull-pen, anyway?'

Mary Ann was aware for the first time that Tony was standing at the bottom of the couch, and she looked at him and back to Mr. Lord and then towards where her ma and da were standing, and she closed her eyes and her mother's voice said, 'Don't make her talk any more just now, Mr. Lord. Please. We'll go into this tomorrow.'

It was a short time later, when upstairs in her bedroom Lizzie was undressing Mary Ann, that she uttered a sharp exclamation and, going to the door, she called softly, 'Mike, here a minute.'

When her da came into the room her mother was standing behind her but she knew she was pointing to her shoulders. She did not know if there were any marks on her shoulders, she only knew that they were paining her, and her neck was so stiff that she could hardly turn her head. Her da's words came on a deep, low tone, as he said, 'What did I tell you? He was shaking her as if he was going to throttle her, and it looks as if he almost done it.' His face came down to hers and he said gently now, 'Does your back hurt, hinnie?'

'Me neck does, Da.'

'Aye.' He patted her cheek. 'Your ma'll rub it for you and it'll be all right in the mornin'.' And now he turned to Lizzie and said, 'And you go off the deep end because I hit him.'

'Well' – Lizzie was speaking quietly now – 'all this to happen after a day like I've had . . . waiting . . . waiting.'

'Your mother didn't turn up?'

'No.'

'Any word why she didn't?'

'No.'

'Huh! Then that's a pleasure we've to look forward to.'

'And your day off wasted.' Lizzie was pulling the clothes up under Mary Ann's chin as she made this statement, and Mary Ann saw a touch of lightness come to her da's face as he looked at her and said, 'Well, I wouldn't say that, not entirely. We had a nice time, didn't we, Mary Ann?'

She tried to nod her head but it was too painful, so she gave him a little smile. She had looked forward all the way home in the bus to telling her mother about the meeting with Mrs. Quinton and how nice her da had been with Mrs. Quinton, but that would have to wait until another time.

CHAPTER FIVE

MRS. McMULLEN

SUNDAY morning found Mary Ann back on the couch in
the kitchen; her neck was so stiff that she could hardly move
it, and her shoulders were very painful . . . and all black and
blue. She had managed to turn her head sufficiently to see a
little of the result of Mr. Johnson's big hands. Her mother
had been for her staying in bed, but she felt too shut out
from everything up there and had begged to be allowed to
lie on the couch in the kitchen. But up to now it hadn't
proved very pleasant, she was not being treated in the light
of an invalid. Their Michael had started things off just before
he took his departure for Mass by remarking with a wide
shake of his head, 'By ! I wonder what you'll trigger off next.
You're the limit, the outside limit. You've got more power for
trouble in you than ten atom bombs.'

'I didn't do anything, our Michael; it wasn't me. I told
me ma; didn't I, Ma?' She appealed to Lizzie's unresponsive
back. 'Lorna Johnson was looking for Tony, and because I
couldn't tell her where he was she swore at me and I went out
and banged the door.' She paused. 'And the latch dropped
and got stuck. It wasn't me.'

'She had a different story. She says you called her in to see
the bull, then ran out and shut the door on her.'

'Oh, the big liar !'

'That's enough of that talk, Mary Ann.'

'But, Ma . . .'

'Enough, I said.'

Then Michael had gone to Mass and her mother had gone
about the business of preparing the Sunday dinner in a

silence which indicated her worried state. Mary Ann sat until nearly dinner-time getting more and more bored, unable to concentrate on reading, and fed-up with the pain in her neck. She wished somebody would come in . . . anybody. Although she hadn't outlined the Sacred Heart on her breast her wish was granted within a matter of minutes. And it brought her upright with such a painful jerk that she brought out, 'Ooh! Oh, Ma !' and her voice trailed away on a sound akin to a groan as her grannie's voice came from the back-door saying, 'Anybody at home ?'

Lizzie was at the oven with her back bent and she seemed to hold the position for a long time although she had closed the oven door, and then she straightened up and looked across the room to where her mother stood in the kitchen doorway, dressed in her Sunday best.

'Well, the place looks as lively as a morgue; not a soul to be seen, only that lad Len. Where's everybody?'

'Oh . . . oh, come in, Mother. Oh, they're about. Michael's gone to Mass.' Lizzie pulled a chair from under the table and said, 'Sit down. Let me have your hat.'

Mrs. McMullen, placing her handbag on the table and slowly taking the pins from her high, black, satin-draped hat, looked towards the couch and Mary Ann and made a cryptic remark. 'Aye ! aye !' she said.

'I was expecting you yesterday, Mother. I thought you might be ill.'

'No, I'm all right, never been fitter. Somebody came in and I couldn't get away. What's wrong with that one ?' She nodded towards the couch as if Mary Ann was a deaf-and-dumb mute who had to be alluded to objectively, and without waiting for Lizzie to reply she handed her her hat and coat and, ignoring the chair that Lizzie had offered, took the one nearest the fire, Mike's particular chair, and sat down.

Lizzie, going towards the hall to deposit her mother's clothes, remarked, 'She had a fall.'

'Aye, I heard about it.'

Lizzie must have thrown the clothes on to the hall table, for she was back in the kitchen within a second, saying,

'You've heard about it? You've been quick, haven't you?' Her voice was curt.

'No, not that you'd notice. I came along the road with that Len. He told me there'd been the devil's figgarties on here last night. He said she'd . . .' there was a bouncing of the head in Mary Ann's direction, 'that she'd locked a lass in with a savage bull and the girl's nearly gone off her rocker, and her father and the noble Mike went at it. And now her father's in hospital with a broken leg and his face all bashed in.'

'Nonsense; he hasn't got a broken leg, it's just his ankle. And his face isn't bashed in.'

'Well, that's what I heard. I'm only repeating what I heard. And don't shout at me, Lizzie. I've only just got in; don't let us start right away.'

As Mrs. McMullen took a neatly folded handkerchief from the pocket of her skirt and, shaking it out, wiped the end of her nose, Lizzie turned towards the table, raising her eyes ceilingwards as she did so. Then, muttering under her breath, 'I won't be a minute', she left the kitchen and Mary Ann at the mercy of her grannie. . . . Or was it the other way about?

The combat would have been equal had Mary Ann been feeling fit, but she was feeling . . . bad. She knew that her mother had gone out to warn her da about the visitor, and she guessed, and rightly, that her grannie had said she was coming yesterday to hoodwink her da, knowing that he would dodge her if he could. She looked now to where her grannie was sitting, her gimlet eyes sending their light across the room, a light which held no trace whatever of affection, and like a young wounded polecat she waited for the old, healthy, wily, ageless cobra to strike. It did.

'Quite a while since you had your name in the papers, isn't it?'

Mary Ann said nothing.

'Must be on three years ago since the country heard of your exploits, when you ran away from that convent. Sussex it was, wasn't it? You got your name on the wireless that time. . . . You've been quiet for a long spell. Most unnatural. . . . Do you know, if the bull had killed that girl they could have hung you?'

On occasions such as this, and there had been a number, and with the same opponent, Mary Ann became vividly aware that she possessed bowels and that there were a lot of them, for the feeling her grannie engendered in her would run up and down and back and forwards all over her stomach. It was an almost indescribable feeling, being a mixture of sickness, aggressiveness, loathing, and desire. It was the ingredient of desire which was at the forefront of her mind at the moment, and she was wishing the old wish yet once again. Oh, if only her grannie would drop down dead. Remembering what Father Owen had said to her on Thursday night about wishes always coming home to roost, she turned her eyes quickly from her grannie's face, and the movement caused a momentary excruciating pain in her neck, and she was reminded of her grannie's words about hanging. But she did not put her hands to her neck, she clapped them on her stomach.

'I shouldn't worry about getting into the paper though, for you'll be in soon enough by the sound of things. That Len said that the man is going to take an action against yer father so he'll have to go to court and you along with him. You'll be in print once more, and that should satisfy you.'

For once Mary Ann could make no rejoinder, she was feeling too awful; her stomach felt as if it was doing somersaults.

'Cat got yer tongue? Or have you realized you've gone too far with this latest escapade and this'll be the finish of you? I wouldn't be surprised if the man claims so much damages that it'll be the finish of him an' all.'

Him did not refer to Mr. Johnson, Mary Ann knew; *him* was her da, and she was stung to retort, 'It wasn't me da's fault. And it wasn't mine either. So there. Len wasn't there and he knows nothing about it. You're always on and trying to make—'

'Mary Ann!' It was her mother speaking as she came into the kitchen. And her grannie's hurt and indignant tone followed up with, 'Oh, don't stop her, she's just showing me her

68

convent manners. But as I told you in the first place, it would take more than a convent to refine her. As for making her talk properly, you have a vain hope there. She's me'ing this and me'ing that as much as ever she did. It's money he's putting down the drain all right in this case. He might as well drink it – he'd have some satisfaction out of it, any rate, then.'

'Now look here, Mother.' Lizzie was standing in front of her mother. 'I've told you before, you're welcome to come to my house at any time, but I won't have you here if you're going to create mischief.'

Mrs. McMullen looked up at her daughter with a pained, hurt expression, and her voice had almost a break in it as she said, 'Well, I like that. I haven't darkened your door for months, and I'm not inside it fifteen minutes and you accuse me of making trouble. Well, I can go the same way as I come; get me my hat and coat. . . .'

As she half rose from the chair Lizzie said, 'Don't be silly, I'm only telling you. I don't want any trouble one way or the other.'

'Well, who's making it? I just open my mouth and make a statement and somebody jumps down my throat.' She did not name the someone but flickered her eyes towards the couch. 'And if there's any complaining to do I can do my share of it. Here I've come all this way and you've never offered me a cup of tea.'

Lizzie sighed. 'The dinner'll be on the table in a few minutes, Mother. . . . All right, I'll make you a cup of tea. Or would you rather have a glass of cider or ginger beer?'

'I'll have a cup of tea if you don't mind, please.' The tone was definite.

Mary Ann watched her mother walk with quick steps to the kitchen. She watched her grannie, after meeting her glance, turn her eyes haughtily away and, leaning her head against the high back of the chair, close her lids as if intending to sleep. Mary Ann, too, lay back against the head of the couch and waited. As she knew her grannie was waiting, waiting until Mike should come in before she started again.

It was nearly half an hour later when they all sat down to

dinner, for Lizzie had had to go for Mike at least three times, and when he eventually entered the kitchen he looked towards Mrs. McMullen and his voice was airy and his glance held nothing out of the ordinary when he said, 'Hullo there.'

Mrs. McMullen did not return the greeting, not verbally at any rate, but inclined her head stiffly towards him.

The first part of the meal was passed over in deceptive friendliness. Mrs. McMullen addressed her remarks to Michael. Mrs. McMullen liked her grandson, and at one time he had liked her, but not so much now, and his answers to her questions about his school career were of such a nature as to have little personal touch in them at all. So the conversation was kept moving mainly between Michael and his grandmother.

It was at the point when Lizzie was asking 'Does anyone want any more meat?' that Mrs. McMullen brought up the subject of horses. It was as if the roast sirloin had in some way reminded her of horses, for she said, 'I suppose you know you've got riding stables opened up not far away?'

'Oh yes.' Lizzie nodded at her mother. 'They've been going about three months now. It's a young fellow that's running them. I hear he's doing well.'

'Yes, he is.' Mrs. McMullen had attacked her fresh supply of sirloin and she kept her eyes directed towards her plate as she made the remark, and it brought the eyes of the others on her as she knew it would.

'Do you know him?' Lizzie's fork was poised half-way to her mouth.

'Yes, yes, I know him. He's young Eddie Travers, Mrs. Flannagan's youngest brother.'

'Oh no.' Lizzie's voice sounded most dismal at this news and Mary Ann, looking at her mother, wondered why she should be so affected by it. She herself was always in some way affected by the name of Flannagan, especially if it had Sarah before it, but why her mother should sound like that she didn't know. That was, not until her da's head went back and he made huh-ing sounds before dropping his head forward again and looking directly at her, saying, 'Well, that's exploded your birthday surprise.'

'Oh, Mike, be quiet!'

'What's the use? Can you see her going taking riding lessons there alongside Miss Sarah Flannagan? They fought in the gutter afore, and there's no reason to think they'll stop if they're on horses. We don't want any horse combats and one or the other breaking their necks.'

Mary Ann was looking at Lizzie now and her eyes were full of disappointment. This then had been the big surprise for her birthday that her mother had hinted at, to take riding lessons. And now it was all nipped in the bud because the man was Sarah Flannagan's uncle. Yet it wasn't against Sarah Flannagan she felt embittered at this moment, but against her grannie. If her grannie hadn't said anything she would likely have gone to the stables and started, and once having started she would have kept on. But now with the knowledge that she was almost sure to run into Sarah, who might already be a horsewoman of some repute – she had a mental vision of Sarah mounted on a large bay, leaping over all the farm gates – she couldn't run that risk. Oh! Her grannie! Her teeth went straight through the crusty top of a baked potato . . . her grannie!

But her grannie had only just begun, she did not show the real reason for her visit until they reached the apple pie and custard. Then her remark-cum-question brought Mary Ann's head up so swiftly that she winced at the pain of her neck as her grannie said, apropos of nothing that had gone before, 'Have you heard the latest about Bob Quinton?'

'Bob?' Lizzie looked full at her mother. 'No, what is it? Has he retired out of the fortune he's made from building?'

'No, it's nothing to do with building. But he's retired all right . . . from his wife.' Mrs. McMullen's round eyes rested now on her daughter and she added, 'It shouldn't surprise you; it didn't me. I've been waitin' for it practically since the day he married.'

'Yes, I can understand that.' Mike's words were slow and definite and brought his mother-in-law's gaze not on to him but directed towards her plate again.

'I don't believe it. Where did you hear that?' There was a

worried note in Lizzie's voice. 'It's just gossip. People will say anything, especially when a couple are happy.'

'What makes you think they were happy?' Mrs. McMullen's small eyes seemed to spring open and upwards towards her daughter. 'They never struck me like that. As for any truth in it, it's true all right because he told me himself.'

'But why?' Lizzie's hands were resting on the table now.

'Because she's a piece, that's why. He could never be happy with a woman like that. Her, a painted—'

'She's not! She's a nice woman, she's beautiful.'

'Mary Ann! Stop that!' Although Lizzie's tone was sharp there was also bewilderment expressed in it. And her bewilderment grew as she looked at Mike as he said, 'Leave her alone, Liz.' Mike's voice was low and even. 'She's only speaking the truth. It's as she says. Connie Quinton's a nice woman, a beautiful woman, and personally I would say that's an understatement.'

'What do you know about her?' Mrs. McMullen's tone was scathing, but Mike answered her with irritating calmness. There was even a touch of laughter in his voice as he replied, 'Well, dear Mother-in-law, more than you think. For your information we had coffee together yesterday morning.'

'Ha! ha! ha!' The ha-ha's were merely an imitation of mirth and Mrs. McMullen followed them up with, 'That's the laugh of the week, that is. You havin' coffee with Connie Quinton. My! my! That'll be the day.'

'He did then. We both had coffee with her and me da and her talked a long time. And she liked him, and she's going to call . . . see!'

'There now, what d'you make of that, eh?' Mike had risen to his feet and had pushed his chair back and was standing looking down at Mrs. McMullen, with a superior smile twisting his lips. 'That's something for you to set the town on fire with, eh? Connie Quinton likes me. Me, Mike Shaughnessy. And she's going to call. Now what d'you make of that, eh? You'd better get on your hat and coat as quick as you can and tell Bob that bit. Go on now. But before you go don't forget to tell Liz' – he lifted his eyes to his wife's amazed face – 'don't forget to tell Liz that you knew this was going to happen and that I'd go off with another woman; in fact you've known I've been carrying on for years, in fact that's why Bob and her split up.'

'I'll not stay in this house and be insulted.'

'No, I wouldn't. And if you hurry you'll just catch the bus at the corner. And, anyway, you'll be quite happy to go, won't you, for you've said all you came to say. Only it didn't have the reaction you hoped for, did it? Ah, well, knowing you, you'll think up something else before very long.' Mike turned from the infuriated glance of his mother-in-law, to turn back leisurely again, adding, 'Oh, and when you're talking to Bob, tell him it's Durrant's we go to.'

Without even casting a glance in Lizzie's direction, Mike now walked out of the kitchen and through the scullery, and they all listened as the back door closed, not with a bang, but just in the ordinary way.

The kitchen was left in a deep, numbing silence. Mary Ann's mind was as full of bewilderment as her mother's face. Her da had called Mrs. Quinton Connie. He had only known her name was Connie because Beatrice had said Aunty Connie, but he had spoken as if he had known her for a long time and had been to Durrant's with her every Saturday. What was the matter with her da? As for her grannie . . . She looked towards the disciple of the devil, who, the picture of offended dignity now, was getting into her coat. Oh, if only something would happen to her grannie, something swift, sure and final.

When a few minutes later Mrs. McMullen, putting the finishing touches to the lapels of her coat and adjusting her hat on a dead straight level, addressed her daughter saying, 'Well, Liz, it'll be a long time afore I darken your door again, you mark my words on that,' Lizzie, standing on the hearthrug, looked at her mother, and all she said was, 'Good-bye, Mother.'

'Good-bye.'

Mrs. McMullen took three steps across the room towards the door, then turned and asked, 'Aren't you comin' to the bus with me?'

'No, Mother, I'm not.'

'Well, now I know where I stand. That's a daughter for you. You can work and slave for years, and what do you get? ... "No, Mother, I'm not. ..." What about you, Michael?'

Michael glared at his grannie but his voice was quiet as he said, 'I'm sorry, but I'm going out with Tony in the car at two o'clock and it's nearly that now.'

'That's a family for you. My God! What is the world coming to? Well, it's as I said—' She swung round to her daughter and, emphasizing her words now with a wag of her finger, she cried, 'It'll be a long time afore you'll see me again.'

She was gone. Lizzie sat down in the chair by the fire but she didn't speak. The table was littered with dishes, but she made no attempt to clear them away, which in itself was unusual, for immediately a meal was finished everything on the table was taken into the scullery.

Mary Ann watched Michael go and stand near her mother and put a tentative hand on her shoulder, saying, 'Don't worry, Mother. Anyway, she won't come back for some time now; you've got that to be thankful for. Come on . . .' He gave her shoulder a little shake, then added, 'I'll dry up for you before I go.'

There were times when Mary Ann liked their Michael, when she liked him very much. She was going to say, 'You go and I'll dry up', even knowing that it had come as anything but a pleasant surprise when he had said he was going out with Tony . . . and in the car. But Lizzie, getting to her feet now, said, 'I'm all right. Get yourself away and don't be late.'

Five minutes later there was only Mary Ann and Lizzie left in the kitchen and the dishes were still on the table, and Lizzie was touching something on the mantelpiece when she said in an off-hand kind of way, 'You did have coffee with Mrs. Quinton yesterday morning, then?'

'Yes, Ma.'

'Why didn't you tell me before?'

'Well, Ma . . .' Mary Ann paused. 'I meant to when I came in, but then . . . then that other thing happened, and

74

this morning my neck was paining and I forgot.'

'Yes, yes, I can see that.' Lizzie started to move the dishes now and Mary Ann watched her face. It had an odd look on it, a look that she had never seen on her mother's face before, not even when she was worried over her da taking a drop.

The true nature of the look on Lizzie's face was not made clear to Mary Ann until that same night when she was in bed and her ma and da were downstairs together waiting for Michael coming in.

She had strained her ears to the low drone of their voices for the past half-hour but had not been able to make anything out, until her mother's voice, rising suddenly, seemed to force its way up through the floorboards below the bed. It brought her into an upright position.

'Well, you could have mentioned it when we got to bed. Or even this morning.'

The words came muffled, and Mary Ann had to bend floorwards to hear them. But there was no need to strain to hear her da's swift reply. 'All right, all right, I'm holding something back. I wasn't just turning the tables on your mother. Have it your own way. I'm starting an affair with her. And why not? Why not indeed?' His voice was higher now. 'I went through hell for years through you and Bob. And now they're splitting up why shouldn't I chance my arm? And don't be like your mother and say I'll be steppin' out of me class, because that doesn't hold in this day and age. And, what's more, the lass is lonely and I wouldn't have to work very hard to get her to accept some comfort. Now, there you've asked for it and you've got it. Are you satisfied now?'

There followed an awe-filled silence when no words came up through the floor, and Mary Ann, with her face cupped in her hands, stared down towards it, waiting. Her body was once more filled with fear and anxiety and she kept saying to herself, 'Oh, Da! Oh, Da!' She knew that her da was being cruel and in a way he was making things up about Mrs. Quinton, and yet there seemed some semblance of truth in what he said. This was brought to her by the picture of her da and Mrs. Quinton sitting looking at each other across the café table. . . . But her da loved her ma; she knew he loved her ma. Then how could he say such awful things? How could he hurt her ma by suggesting that he would go off with Mrs. Quinton? The whole situation had turned topsy-turvy. It was Mr. Quinton she had been afraid of coming after her ma again.

Thoughts of Mr. Quinton and her ma led her back to what she had overheard while standing in the brush cupboard last Saturday afternoon, and there seemed a similarity between what Mrs. Quinton had said about the row she had had with her husband and her da and ma going at it in the kitchen now. Or was it what Mrs. Willoughby had said? Mrs. Willoughby had said, 'I know you, Connie; you keep on and on.' And that's what her ma had been doing, keeping on and on.

And when she heard the back-door bang Mary Ann knew that her da was doing what Mr. Quinton had done, walking out. But her da would go no farther than the farm. Or would he go walking round thinking of Mrs. Quinton and then . . .

She was out of bed and down the stairs within a matter of seconds.

Lizzie was sitting at the kitchen table, her face buried in the crook of her elbow, and though she made no sound Mary Ann knew that she was crying bitterly.

'Ma. Oh, Ma!'

Lizzie's head came up with a start, but she did not look at her daughter; she kept her face turned away as she said, 'Now what do you want? You should be in bed.'

'Ma, Mrs. Quinton doesn't want . . .'

Lizzie was on her feet glowering now. 'Get back to bed. You'll keep your ears open once too often, milady. Go on upstairs this minute with you. And don't let me hear you mention Mrs. Quinton's name in this house again. Do you hear?'

Mary Ann, her head drooped, turned away and walked slowly upstairs. She had been going to tell her ma that Mrs. Quinton didn't want her da, she only wanted Mr. Quinton. She had been going to tell her what she had heard from the brush cupboard, but Lizzie's manner had indicated to her plainly that she had taken a dislike to Mrs. Quinton and that being so it was not likely that she would believe anything nice about her.

As Mary Ann stood at her bedroom window and looked out on to the dark shape of the farmyard, screwing up her eyes in the hope of catching a glimpse of her da, she knew that the three years of peace had suddenly slid out of life as if they had never been, and the old pattern had returned. It only wanted her da to go and get . . . she halted her mind on the thought. She would not even think that it only wanted Mike to go and get drunk for life to be as it was.

Her eyes lifted from the yard to the sky and in a vague way she realized she was changing, and the realization was forced upon her by the clarity with which she was seeing the position between her parents and the Quintons. And she was saddened by the knowledge that the more people loved, the more intensely could they hurt and be hurt, and as she turned from the window and groped her way to the bed she wished with a deep solemn wish that she need never grow up.

CHAPTER SIX

MR. LORD LOOKS AHEAD

ON the following morning Mary Ann came downstairs feeling like nothing on earth. When she was in bed her ma had asked her how she felt and she had said, 'All right', but now she was up her neck was paining her and, what was most unusual, she didn't want to go to school.

On entering the kitchen she was going to tell her mother this when she was stopped by the sight of Tony. He was already dressed for the office, and he was talking to her da and did not pause to look at her when she entered the room but went on saying, 'And the latest is, I've got to promise I won't marry for five years . . . or else. I have no intention of marrying yet awhile, but to make such a promise is another thing.'

'Oh, it's all on account of this Lorna business. I wouldn't lay too much stock on what he says at the moment.'

Mary Ann noticed that this morning her da did not sound as interested as usual in Tony's problems, from which she gathered that her ma and him hadn't made it up. But her ma's voice was kind, even gentle, when, looking at her, she asked, 'Is your neck paining you now?'

'Yes, Ma, it's very sore.'

'Well, you'd better not go to school this morning.'

'All right, Ma.'

Tony caught her attention again but not very strongly as he said to Mike, 'And when I said to him, "And I suppose you'll want to pick who I'm to marry?" he said quite flatly, "Yes, you can rest assured that'll be more than likely".' She found she couldn't work up the interest the situation between

Tony and Mr. Lord warranted. The pain in her neck was making her feel a bit sick and there was the business of her ma and da.

Lizzie bent over Mary Ann now, saying, 'Aren't you going to eat your cereal?'

'No, Ma. I don't want anything.'

On this Mike spoke to Lizzie without looking at her. 'You'd better get her to the doctor's,' he said.

'Yes, that would be a wise move at this point.' On Tony's words Mike looked at him inquiringly but did not speak, and Tony, taking his glance from Mike for a moment, said, 'That's really why I popped in, to warn you. They're going to take the matter to court.'

'What!' The exclamation came from Lizzie.

'Yes,' said Tony. 'They are going to make it assault and loss of work for both of them.' His voice was very low as he gave this information, and Lizzie, perhaps for the first time that morning, looked at her husband. Mike did not return the look, but his head went up and he said, 'Let them. Let them do their damnedest. I've got a case to put an' all.' Then his chin coming in, he turned his head sharply to Tony and demanded, 'You still seeing that one?'

'No, I'm not, Mike.' Tony spoke definitely. 'She made it her business last night to waylay me and she gave me this information, hoping, I think, that I'd try to persuade her father not to take any measures against you. But you know what that would mean, don't you, and I thought you'd rather have things as they stand now.'

'Aye, damn, yes. Don't you go putting your head into a noose because of me. You did right there. And take my advice and give her a clear road.'

'Well, once they've left the place it won't be difficult, but at the moment I seem to stumble over her at every step I take. I'm sorry about all this, Mike; it's really my fault, as you said, taking her out in the first place.'

Mary Ann felt no relief at Tony's changed attitude towards Lorna Johnson. Even the prospect of being taken to court did not reach the gigantic proportions of the situation that was now in existence between her parents. The situation that spread its atmosphere through the kitchen and which could be felt by everybody, Tony and Michael included, and Michael ate his breakfast in a questioning silence that caused his eyes to flicker every now and again between his parents.

From the window of his office Mike saw Mary Ann and Lizzie pass the gate. Mary Ann looked into the farmyard but not Lizzie, her gaze was directed straight ahead, and Mike said, 'Blast, damn and blast.' What he wanted to do was dash after them, pull Lizzie round to him, look into her eyes and say, 'Aw lass, come on, come on. Now ask yourself, now ask yourself, is there anybody on God's earth for me but you?' He had said similar words to her three years ago when she had got worked up over the Polinski girl. It was odd, but he had never even given her cause to be jealous. That was one thing he hadn't got on his conscience. Now he himself had had cause to be jealous, for at one time Bob Quinton was never off the doorstep, waiting for the moment she was going to walk out. He rubbed his hand roughly around his face. He supposed he shouldn't have said what he did to the old girl yesterday, it must have sounded a bit odd. But the chance to get one over on that old devil had been too much for him. He realized he had made more out of his acquaintance with Mrs. Quinton than was necessary, and he wouldn't for the world have done it if he had thought Liz was going to take it in the way she had. He expected her to laugh over it. But then he should have had the sense to know that women don't laugh at the same things as men. The trouble was that once this kind of rift got hold you never knew where it would end. In some cases it split the lives in two with the shock of an earthquake, in others it just spread unobtrusively like a malignant disease, until one morning you woke up petrified with what had hit you.

His elbows on the desk, he brought his head on to his good hand, and it was in this position that Mr. Lord came upon him and said abruptly, 'Hullo, what's the matter? Under the weather?'

Mike got hastily to his feet, answering as he did so, 'No, sir. I just happened to be thinking for a minute.'

The old man stared into Mike's big face, his eyes narrowed and penetrating. He stared until Mike, moving uneasily, asked, 'Anything up, sir?'

'That's what I would like to hear from you.'

'Me? I don't know what you're getting at. Are you referring to Saturday night's business?'

'No, I'm not referring to Saturday night's business. I happen to be referring to the situation between you and your wife.'

Every feature in Mike's face became stiff, but before he could make any retort Mr. Lord put in, 'And don't tell me it isn't any of my business. If you shout your business loud enough for people coming to your door to hear what is being said, it is no longer your own business.'

'What are you talking about?' Mike's expression was now one of bewilderment.

'I happened to call on you last evening for the purpose of inquiring if Tony had returned home. You were going at it so hard that I heard every word you said when I was yards away from the door. . . . This woman Connie Quinton, what about her?'

Mike seemed to reach half his height again and there was quite an interval before he spoke, and then his words came low and dangerously deep as he said, 'Now look you here, sir, I'm not unaware of what I owe you, and I repay you with my work from dawn, many days until dusk. Aye and later. And I repay you with my loyalty and with trying to save every shilling I can for you. But there you have all of my life you have any right to; the rest is my concern. Do you hear me, sir? What happens behind them walls over there—' He now worked his thumb vigorously over his shoulder. '—what happens within them walls concerns me and my wife.'

Mr. Lord was staring fixedly at Mike all the time he was speaking, and now his gaze dropped away for a moment as he said in an extraordinarily calm tone, 'I've always admired you for one thing, Shaughnessy: you speak your mind. And I had found that you speak the truth. But you can't intimidate me with this manner of yours about the sanctity of your married life. Your wife is troubled. I like your wife, she's a very fine woman, and I don't want to see you playing ducks and drakes—'

'Look, sir.' Mike was trying to keep his temper under control. 'This is all a mountain out of a mole-hill.'

'It didn't sound like that to me. Nor would it have done so to anyone else who was passing your house last night. It sounded as if you were having an affair with this woman and your wife had found out. Is she, by any chance, the wife of Quinton the builder . . . my builder?' He motioned his head in the direction of his house.

'Yes, she is. And I'm not having an affair with her.' Mike paused to draw in breath through his teeth. 'God in Heaven, I met the woman on Saturday morning in a café when Mary Ann and I went in for a cup of coffee. I'd never clapped eyes on her before. She happens to be the aunt of Mary Ann's school pal. We spoke for ten minutes or so, and that's the beginning and the end of it as far as I'm concerned. Look, sir' – Mike's voice became slow and patient sounding – 'it was like this . . .'

For the next few minutes Mike explained what had occurred on Mrs. McMullen's visit yesterday, and the explanation seemed to satisfy Mr. Lord. It even seemed to give him some slight amusement, for the muscles of his face twitched as he listened. And when Mike had finished he said, 'Well, if that's the case you must make it up with Mrs. Shaughnessy and let's have no more of this. We've enough trouble on our hands without domestic ones. Now about Johnson.' He jerked his head in a bird-like fashion before going on. 'The wife has just been up to me. She means to make the most out of it. They're taking the matter to a solicitor. That means court, unless you come to some arrangement and pay what they ask. Have you any money saved?'

'About ninety pounds.'

'Huh! Well, that won't go far. If it reaches court those sharks'll have that in the first lick if you lose; and let me tell you, as I see things you are likely to. Blast the man! And his family!' Mr. Lord's face now became stiff, as did his voice, as he went on, 'I never liked him from the day he came. . . .'

Now don't say it. Don't say it. I know I engaged him myself, but I still maintain I've never liked him, and the sooner he's gone the better. The sooner they're all gone the better. As things stand I think it's just as well he's taking the matter to court because if he didn't he would expect to carry on here as usual, and I don't want him here. I want them gone as soon as possible. You understand?'

'Yes, sir, I understand.'

Mr. Lord turned and looked away from Mike and out of the office window, and now he said, 'You seem to do a lot of talking to Tony, and him to you. What does he think about this girl?' The last two words were rapped out.

'I don't think you need to worry in that direction – that is, if you don't pull the reins too tight. He's a man, he's not a lad any longer, and you've got to recognize this and let him go his own road.'

Mr. Lord swung his gaze from the window on to Mike, repeating as he did so, 'Own road? That's just what I won't let him do, and finish at a dead end. That's where young men finish who are let go their own road. Dead ends. Look, Shaughnessy, I'm going to speak frankly to you. There are very few people whom I can say that to, but you're concerned in this particular matter as much as I am. . . . Yes, you can look surprised, but whatever tight rein I hold on him will ultimately be for your benefit as well as my own, you and yours. Do you follow me?'

Mike's eyes were screwed up as he peered at the old man and he said quietly now, 'No, sir, I'm afraid I don't. I can't very well see what Tony's future has got to do with me.'

'I said you and yours.' The two men were staring at each other, and in the silence that fell on them could be heard the lowing of the cows in the byre and the purring of a tractor in a far field. And then Mr. Lord said, 'Little girls grow up. In five years' time Mary Ann will be seventeen. Now do you understand me?'

Yes. Yes, Mike understood and he was shocked with his understanding. The shock was overlaying his surprise and was so great that for a moment he couldn't speak. And Mr. Lord said, 'My life went wrong. I've had very few interests in my time, that is until I met your child, and from then things seemed to happen to me – I built a house where I had never intended building a house, then Tony came and everything was completely changed. I'm old, but not too old still to have desires and dreams, and my main desire, my one dream, is to see that my grandson gets the right woman. You should take it as a compliment, Shaughnessy, that I'm picking on your daughter, for, after all, she's two-thirds you. But I see that it isn't affecting you that way. Now, now' – he raised his hand firmly in front of Mike's face – 'don't say it. Not now, for you'll likely tell me you'd see me in hell first before you would let me have my own way. Well, that is what I'd expect you to say, but I don't want to hear it. The only thing I'm asking you is to remember that I trust you, and as yet Tony must know nothing of this. I'll tell him when the time is ripe. Now I must away.' He looked at his watch, and without any word of good-bye he left Mike with a face as red as his hair. . . .

Mike slowly sat down on the office stool. He couldn't find words, not even strong ones, to use as an exclamation to fit the old man's audacity. After a moment he said to himself: 'What can you say?' A few minutes ago he had been worrying about the state of affairs between him and Liz, and now here it had been told to him, and by no other than the old boy himself, who was worth God knows what, that he proposed keeping his grandson and heir free until Mary Ann was of an age to marry. It was fantastic. But even 'fantastic' didn't seem to fit the situation. It was somehow . . . shocking, even indecent in a way. Mary Ann, a child of twelve, well, near thirteen, and Tony already twenty-three. How would Tony take it when he found out what was in the old man's mind? Pack up and go off – and likely marry the first girl that came his way just to show the old boy who was master of his fate. And who could blame him?

And then there was Mary Ann. How would she react in five years' time? Would she be a different Mary Ann? Of one thing he was certain: she wouldn't be so changed that if she wanted Tony and he was still available there would be no obstacle she wouldn't remove to have him. But, on the other hand, if she didn't want Tony nobody on God's earth would be able to make her take him. The odds seemed to lie with Mary Ann.

Mike raised his head and looked out of the open doorway to where in the far distance a cloud of dust coming down the hill indicated that Mr. Lord was on his way to town. Yet it wasn't of the old man that Mike thought as he watched the car disappear, but strangely it was of Corny Boyle. Mary Ann, used as she was now to Tony, and acquainted with the gracious living that was the daily routine in the house on the hill, also mixing daily with the class that she met in the convent, had asked to her party Corny Boyle. Yes, the decision would lie with Mary Ann.

This was a very relieving thought, and it pushed Mike's head back and he smiled and gave a little relieved ha-ha of a laugh before getting up from the stool and going about his work.

No bones broken, was the doctor's report on Mary Ann. The pain in her neck was from the bruises, about which he remarked that it looked as if she had been clutched by a gorilla.

Mary Ann repeated the doctor's remark to Mike at dinnertime and he said, 'We must remember that.'

Mary Ann was puzzled by Mike's attitude when she returned home. He wasn't mad any more and he was making an effort to get her ma round. But this appeared to be fruitless. At odd times during their dinner she found him looking at her, not the way he did when he was vexed or yet pleased, but in a way she couldn't make out.

During the afternoon she felt better, and because of this the time began to drag. She was reluctant to go round the farmyard after Saturday night's business. She had a greater reluctance about paying a visit to Mr. Lord. She did think that she might wander up and talk to Ben. But then she didn't know if Mr. Lord was in or out. So by four o'clock she was wishing heartily for the morrow when she would be back at school again, and thinking of school she decided to go to the main road and meet Michael coming off the bus.

This would undoubtedly surprise him, but she was thinking less of that than of the excursion giving her something to do.

She had just gone a short way along the road when she heard the wireless playing. She knew it was the Johnsons' wireless and they would be sitting in the garden with the window open. She hadn't seen any of the Johnsons since Saturday night and she was afraid of meeting them now, yet at the same time she was glad they were in the garden, for she had something to say to Lorna Johnson.

Mrs. Johnson and her daughter were sitting in deck-chairs on the tiny square of lawn below the cottage window. Mrs. Johnson was knitting and Lorna was reclining with her hands behind her head. That was, until she caught sight of Mary Ann, when she sat bolt upright. Mrs. Johnson, too, sat upright, and putting the knitting on the grass, she rose to her feet and walked a few steps to the railings that separated her from Mary Ann, and over them she greeted her with, 'You! You damned little bitch! You know what I'd like to do with you?'

Mary Ann stopped in the middle of the road and looked at Mrs. Johnson. You weren't supposed to answer grown-ups back, so, taking her eyes from Mrs. Johnson's angry dark face, she looked to where Lorna was still sitting in the chair and she said quietly, 'I didn't lock you in with the bull, and I never asked you into the byre. You know I didn't. You came in yourself, you know you did. You were looking for—'

'Shut up your mouth and get yourself on your way before I forget meself and slap the face off you.' Mrs. Johnson looked as if she could carry out her threat any minute, and Mary Ann, who was backing away and looking at Mrs. Johnson now, said, 'Well, I didn't lock her in; it's all lies.'

'Yes, you did.' Lorna had joined her mother. 'Ooh! You little rat, when I think what you've done!' Lorna's lips were wide apart and her teeth were tightly clenched, and it looked for the moment as if she was going to have another screaming fit, when her mother commanded sharply, 'That's enough. Say no more, keep it for the court. Go on, get yourself away, you.' Mrs. Johnson flung her arm wide as if to swipe Mary

Ann from the face of the earth, and Mary Ann turned and got herself away and in a hurry. She was trembling and more than a little afraid. The viciousness of the Johnson woman was something that she hadn't encountered before.

When she came within sight of the main road but still some way off she recognized the boy standing on the verge near the main road as their Michael, for his figure was similar to that of her da, only in smaller proportions. But what brought her almost to a stop was the fact that Michael was not alone. He was standing talking to a girl, and the girl was sitting on a pony with her back to Mary Ann.

Mary Ann had never seen Michael talking to a girl; Michael didn't like girls. Her step became slower, her curiosity deepened. Their Michael knew a girl with a horse. His prestige mounted . . . until she came silently within a few yards of them and they, still intent with each other, did not hear her coming. Even before Mary Ann halted, the amazing revelation was working its way with furious indignation up through her body. The girl on the horse was not in jodhpurs but in jeans, and topping the jeans was a red sweater, and lying down the back of the red sweater was a long black pony-tail of hair. It was the hair style that had deceived her; she would have known that back in a million if it hadn't been for the hair style.

The ferocity of her feelings must have reached the pair in front of her, for as Michael turned his head sharply in Mary Ann's direction Sarah Flannagan swung her slim waist round in the saddle.

In three years Sarah Flannagan had changed mightily. She was a tall, slim girl with attractive dark looks and appeared much older than fourteen. The manner in which she handled the meeting with her life-long enemy bore this out, for with a wry smile on her face she looked down on the diminutive figure and said with disarming casualness, 'Hullo, Mary Ann.'

It was an approach that would have taken a strong wind out of a galleon's sails and it stumped Mary Ann. Never before had she heard Sarah Flannagan speak in a voice like that to her, or anyone else for that matter. Mary Ann was quick to recognize immediately that gone was the girl who used to taunt her and walk behind her chanting:

> 'Swanky Shaughnessy – there she goes:
> Two boss eyes and turned-in toes;
> She cannot even wipe her nose,
> Swanky Shaughnessy – there she goes.'

Or the edifying rhyme which went:

> 'Pig's belly,
> Wobble Jelly;
> Pig's fat,
> Dirty cat.
> Pig's skin,
> Double chin;
> Pig's cheek,
> Shiny beak.
> Pig's lug,
> Ugly mug—
> And that's Mary Ann Shaughnessy.'

But Mary Ann remembered. Yet not because of the insults hurled at herself. Those didn't matter. What did matter was that this girl had been the main taunt of her life where her da was concerned. Had she not written up on a wall for all to see:

MARY ANN SHAUGHNESSY IS A BIG LIAR AND HER DA'S A DRUNKEN NO-GOOD AND EVERYBODY KNOWS IT.

So to Sarah's greeting she answered not at all, but, turning her stiff, indignant glance on her brother, she said, 'Our Michael!' and in those two words was conveyed all the recrimination that his disloyalty warranted.

Michael, his face one large blush now, demanded, 'What's up with you?'

What could Mary Ann answer to this but, 'I'll tell me ma.'

'Go on, tell her. Go on, nobody's stopping you.'

Mary Ann, floundering now in a situation of which she hadn't had time to get the measure, turned her eyes upwards again towards Sarah and with something like the flavour from the old battle-field she demanded, 'What you doing here, anyway? This is our place.'

'Oh, be your age.' This scathing and cool remark brought Mary Ann's chin rearing upwards, but before she could say anything Sarah in a changed tone added, 'We are not kids in Burton Street any more; why can't you forget about them days?'

It was as if an adult was chastising her. It was most unsettling and it would have deflated her entirely had she not grasped at one flaw in the seemingly superior poise of her old enemy. Sarah Flannagan had said 'them' instead of 'those'; she didn't speak properly. Slowly now and with Sister Catherine's tuition well to the fore, she looked directly up into Sarah's face and ejaculated – 'said' could never describe her next words – 'I-am-bee-ing-my-age, and-no-matter-how-old-I-grow-I-shall-never-forget-what-you-have-said-about... my father.'

It was as surprising to herself as to her listeners to hear her refer to Mike as 'my father'. 'Me da' was synonymous with her feelings and claim to Mike as a parent; 'my father' was a word used by other children for other men.

Sarah, without raising her voice, said, 'All right, I'm not denying it.'

'Well then!'

'Well then, what about it?'

'You were always a liar.'

On this statement a change came over Sarah's face and she looked more recognizable to Mary Ann. In another minute they would have been back on their old footing had not Sarah's desire for peace, instigated, it must be confessed, by her acquaintance with Michael and her hopes for its continuance, made her turn what could have been a damning remark merely into an offensive one by saying, 'Well, you could do your share. And, anyway, what I said was true, wasn't it?'

'It wasn't!' The denial was definite.

'Oh, come off it, Mary Ann; you can't hoodwink yourself any more. And what is it, anyway, getting drunk?'

'He didn't. He never got drunk.'

'Shut up and don't be so stupid.' Michael's indignant tone brought Mary Ann round to him, and Michael, towering over her now, his voice nearly as deep as Mike's, said, 'Sarah's right. Be your age. You know he drank like a fish, and would now if it wasn't for—'

'Shut up, you! I'll slap your face, our Michael, if you don't shut up.'

Michael shut up, and he boiled with rage as he shut up. It wasn't the knowledge that she had a sore neck and shoulders that kept his hands off her, but he didn't want to make a spectacle of himself in front of Sarah. And now Sarah, from her superior height, poured warm oil on the troubled waters, for she said quickly, 'What does it matter about your da drinking; mine drinks like three dry Scotsmen. He has from that Coronation night when he went out with your da. . . . Oh yes' – she laughed down on Mary Ann now – 'if you're holding things against people, I should hold that against you, for it was from that night he started drinking, and heavily. But there' – her head wagged – 'I don't hold drinking against me da, because he's able to hold his own against me mother now more than he ever did afore and that's a good thing. Me mother's not half the tartar she was.'

Mary Ann's face was undergoing alterations, she was staring up at this Sarah Flannagan, at this new Sarah Flannagan, who was saying she didn't mind her da drinking, and was saying that she knew her mother was a tartar. Then Sarah brought Mary Ann's mouth into an even bigger gape when she said, 'I'm getting away from home as soon as I can. When I leave school at the end of the summer Burton Street won't see me. I'm coming out here to work in the stables for my uncle – I love horses.' She turned her eyes now on to the pony's neck and stroked its mane for a moment before looking down, not on to Mary Ann now, but on to Michael, and saying without any preamble, 'I've had 'flu. I'm off school for a week and me uncle lets me exercise the horses if they haven't been out during the day. You can come over any night and help if you like.' Then without waiting for Michael's answer she said, 'So long now.' Flicking her gaze next to Mary Ann, she said, 'So long, Mary Ann.' With a tap of her heels into the pony's flanks she was off, leaving two strangely disturbed people behind her.

Well, to talk to their Michael like that, to ask him to come and see her like that, pretending that it was to take the horses out. Well! Mary Ann had to find something to dislike this new Sarah Flannagan for. She couldn't, not all in one go, turn the enemy of her life into a friend. Friend! That would be the day. Tolerable acquaintance would be more fitting the mark. And their Michael to talk to her . . . to even want to talk to Sarah Flannagan. And he did – she could tell by his face that he wanted to talk to her. She turned and looked now at her brother, but her brother was looking at the heels of the pony and its rider who was disappearing round the bend of the road, and from his expression Mary Ann knew to her shocked amazement that their Michael was 'gone on Sarah Flannagan'. Wait until her ma heard that.

It would seem that Michael had heard her thoughts, for he turned on her violently now, saying, 'Go on, what's stopping you now; get home and spill the beans. And let me tell you something.' He stooped from his height and dug his finger into her narrow chest. 'If you were as sensible as Sarah Flannagan you would do; and, what's more, there wouldn't be half the trouble going on – see?'

She had come to meet their Michael off the bus – it had been a nice thought in its origin – and now she had met him, and all she wanted to do was to lash out and kick his shins. But, as last night, she realized she was growing older. And now as she watched Michael's indignant back moving swiftly away from her she realized, too, that lashing out and kicking shins as a form of retaliation was also gone. Gone with the years of 'Pig's belly: Wobble jelly', with 'Swanky Shaughnessy, There she goes', with

> 'Boxy, boxy,
> Push it down your socksy;
> Umper, umper, push it up your jumper.'

The world was changing, her world was changing, she didn't feel like herself any more. Slowly, and keeping a good distance behind Michael, she made her way home.

What impression Michael's news had on their mother Mary Ann did not know because she hadn't been present when he told her. That he had told her she was positively sure because it was confirmed as soon as her da entered the kitchen, for turning to his father, Michael said, 'Da, I've been talking to Sarah Flannagan at the end of the road; is there anything wrong in that?'

Mike looked at his son for a moment, then repeated, 'Sarah Flannagan? Here? What's she after?'

'She was exercising one of the ponies – her uncle's ponies.'

'Ooh.' Mike flicked his eyes in Mary Ann's direction. She was waiting for his glance but could make nothing of it. And then Michael said, 'And she's asked me to go along there and help if I want to.'

'Do you want to?'

Michael's eyelids flickered before he said. 'Well, yes, yes I do.'

'Well, there's no reason why you shouldn't, is there? That is if you get your homework done.'

Mike and his son looked at each other for a space, and then Mike, with a wry smile to his lips, said, 'Enjoy yourself. And it's a good way to start – with horses.'

With horses! Her da had said nothing about Sarah Flannagan, nothing that he should say. And her mother had said nothing. People were funny. Everything was very funny at the present time, and it wasn't funny ha-ha either.

CHAPTER SEVEN

DIPLOMACY

ALMOST invariably Mike's mail consisted of bills in thin brown envelopes or of catalogues. The latter he would peruse during breakfast, commenting on their nature to Lizzie with such remarks as: 'They are on about immunizing the calves against husk. Better be safe than sorry, I suppose', or 'I think I'll try these Conder people for seeds for the barley'. But never had Mary Ann known him to read a letter then put it in his pocket, which was what he had just done. The envelope had been typed, she had noticed this as she watched him slit it open, and some change in his expression as he looked at the letter caused her to keep her eyes on him. And when he had finished it she watched him slowly fold it up and place it in his back trouser pocket, for he hadn't a coat on. Her mother, too, had noticed this, and under ordinary circumstances would have said, 'What's that about?' But Mary Ann knew that although her mother spoke to her da in front of them she was still . . . not kind with him, and this prevented her from asking about the letter.

Then at the end of breakfast Mike said something that chilled Mary Ann's heart, and her mother's too, for she saw her mother's face turn a greyish colour when her da said, 'I'll have to be slipping out this mornin'. I'll go and see to Len and Jonesy and then I'll be off.' With this, he pulled on his working coat and left the kitchen.

Mary Ann looked at their Michael, but Michael was looking at their mother, and Lizzie was looking out of the kitchen window watching her husband stride down the path towards the gate.

93

This was Saturday. Her da had taken his day off yesterday as usual. What had he to go out for . . . into Newcastle for? She felt that Newcastle was his destination. Was he going to see . . . ? She would not even say the name to herself, but she saw the face of Mrs. Quinton smiling under her smart white hat and, as always when anxiety hit her, it registered in her stomach and for a moment she felt sick. And her mother felt sick, too. She could tell by her face that she felt sick.

But Lizzie's expression now was nothing compared to the look on her face when, half an hour later, Mike came down-stairs dressed in his best suit. He glanced in the mirror and pulled his tie straight before saying, 'I'll be off now.'

Her face was half turned from him and her voice was low as she asked, 'Will you be long?'

'No, I don't suppose so.' He bent his head and kissed her cheek and she never moved.

Mary Ann had not asked, 'Can I go with you, Da?' It was Saturday morning and she had nothing to do, but she hadn't asked a question that she knew would be useless. And when he went out without bidding her a good-bye she felt as if her world had come to an end. The feeling she was experiencing was even worse than at those times in the past when he had gone out to get full. In a way she knew how to cope with drink, experience had taught her so much, but a woman was different. Mrs. Quinton had said she loved her husband. Then why was she going after her da? Perhaps she wasn't, perhaps the letter wasn't from her. The feeling in Mary Ann's breast held out no hope that she was mistaken. She sat in the kitchen, her face the picture of misery, until some time later Lizzie, turning on her sharply, said, 'Don't sit there looking like that, get yourself out to play.'

'I don't want to play, Ma. And, anyway, there's nobody to play with.'

'Well, go and do something. Do your homework or any-thing, but don't sit there looking like that.'

When Mary Ann got to her feet and stood hesitating whether to go outside or upstairs Lizzie said suddenly, 'You can get your things on and go to Mrs. McBride's and take her some eggs and things.'

Another time she would have jumped for joy at being allowed to go to Mrs. McBride's, particularly as her mother had been doing her best to keep her away from Mulhattan's Hall and the district. But this morning it brought her no joy. Silently she went upstairs and put on her coat, brushed her hair and was about to tie it back with a ribbon when she remembered the pony-tail hanging down Sarah Flannagan's back. So she left it swinging loose. Then returning to the kitchen, she took the basket from the table and her bus fare from her mother, and without any other word but a dull, 'Bye-bye, Ma', she left the house.

Coming dolefully to the main road, Mary Ann discovered she had lost the bus she usually took into Jarrow, so she caught the next one. The route was a little longer but would get her there just the same.

She had been travelling in the bus about fifteen minutes and was passing an open space where a factory was under construction when her interest was quickened by seeing in large letters the name that was actually filling her mind at the moment. It was heading a hoarding which said simply: ROBERT QUINTON – BUILDER AND CONTRACTOR. The hoarding drew her eyes like a magnet and she twisted around in her seat to catch a last glimpse of it.

When she alighted at the next stop she did not remember having made the decision, the advisability of which she questioned by saying to herself, 'It's Saturday, there'll be nobody about.' The glimpse she had had of the place had shown her no one at work. But as she walked back up the road towards the main entrance she said to herself, 'There'll be a watchman or someone and he'll tell me when he'll be there.' The last 'he' referred to Mr. Robert Quinton, Builder and Contractor. Had she been asked she would have been unable to tell you when the thought of going to see Bob had entered her mind. Now that it was in and firmly fixed, see him she must.

The enclosure was a mass of bricks, girders, and machinery surrounding the skeleton of a large factory, with a row of prefab. buildings to the side of it. There was no sign of a watchman. In fact, there was no sign of a living soul about the place. A notice which had the single word 'Office' and an arrow on it led her around a pile of rubble, under the arm of a gigantic grab, and behind a cement-mixer, and there she saw the building. It was the last of the line of prefab. structures. It had one window and this was almost taken up by a man's back – likely the watchman's.

Making hastily for the door and not looking where she was placing her feet, she tripped and almost fell. She just saved the basket from scattering its contents, but sent an empty tin drum, which she had grabbed in an effort to save herself, clattering amongst a heap of iron. When she was upright once again and facing the window the back had disappeared, and before she reached the office door it was opened. And there stood Bob Quinton himself.

'Well, well, Mary Ann. What ... what are you doing here?'

She saw that Mr. Quinton was surprised to see her, and also that he was slightly agitated.

'I wanted to see you and I was looking for the watchman to ask him. .... I didn't think you'd be here when they're not working.'

'Oh, I'm usually around when there's no work to do.' He laughed as if he had made a great joke, then stopped abruptly. Looking down on her, he said, 'It's a long time since we met, Mary Ann – you haven't changed much.'

This was a way of telling her that she hadn't grown. She said, 'I'll be thirteen on the first of June.'

'Will you indeed? Time does fly, doesn't it?' He moved from one foot to the other, and rubbed his hands together. His actions spoke of his unease, and this somehow strengthened Mary Ann's courage and she said quietly but quite firmly, 'I would like to talk to you, Mr. Quinton.'

'You would?'

'Yes ... yes, please.'

'Oh.' Now his unease mounted to almost agitation and he said, 'Well now, well now, I'm – I'm rather full up with work, clerical work, you know.'

'I won't keep you, if I could come in just for a minute?'

There were two reasons why she wanted to enter the office:

first, to be able to put the basket down some place safely, preferably on a level floor; second, her legs were beginning to shake and she wanted to sit down.

But her request seemed to throw Mr. Quinton into a dither, and if Mary Ann hadn't known she had left her mother safely at home, she would have thought Mr. Quinton had her in his office, and so did not want to let her go in. But when after a minute or so and a big intake of breath Mr. Quinton stood aside and without speaking allowed her to enter the office, she found it quite empty.

Thankfully she placed the basket on the floor, and without waiting for a formal invitation she sat down. Then, without any preamble as was her way when dealing with important things, she came straight to the point, saying, 'I was at Beatrice Willoughby's party a week past Saturday and I met your – I met Mrs. Quinton.'

Mr. Quinton, knowing something of Mary Ann's past history, remained quiet, but seemingly even more agitated, for his eyes ranged round the room, and at one time Mary Ann was surprised to see him biting on the side of his fore-finger. He had turned his gaze completely away from her when she said, 'We were playing hide-and-seek. I was in the brush cupboard in the kitchen and I heard Mrs. . . . Mrs. Quinton and Mrs. Willoughby talking. They were talking about you and . . . and me ma, Mr. Quinton.'

Bob's head jerked round towards her even while his body was turned from her. And, looking at him standing in this strained position, she went on, 'And I felt sick and had to come out of the cupboard. And Mrs. Quinton held my head, and after we got talking and she told me something.'

Bob was facing Mary Ann now and he had his eyes closed, and he said, weakly, even pleadingly, 'Mary Ann.' Her name spoken in such a tone was a plea for her to stop, but she didn't stop, she hadn't reached the important point of her mission yet, she was coming to it. Ignoring the plea, she went on with quiet resolution. 'She said she liked you . . . she liked you very much, the same way as me ma likes me da.'

Bob Quinton now put his hand out backwards and, grabbing at a seat, swung it round. Then, dropping on to it, he faced Mary Ann. But all he said was, 'Oh, Mary Ann', in a tone one would say, 'My dear, my dear'. And encouraged, she went on more quickly now, and, sensing an advantage, she let her imagination have full play by adding, 'Mrs. Quinton was crying' – this at least was true – 'and she said that she was silly and jealous and she couldn't help going on and on about a thing and it got on your nerves. But that she still liked you – and she would always like you, forever.'

Bob Quinton's head was bowed and his lids lowered and his face had a sad look and Mary Ann found that she was liking him. She refrained from referring to the other point of the triangle, that of Mike and his supposed infatuation for Mrs. Quinton, for reason told her that if Mr. Quinton went back to his wife that would put paid to her da. Mr. Quinton couldn't know anything about this part and what you didn't know couldn't do you any harm. That was Mrs. McBride's saying. Even as bad as she knew her grannie to be, she didn't think she was bad enough to go and tell him what had taken place on Sunday. So surely it was better to let some sleeping dogs lie while rousing others, so she said, 'Me ma's so proud of me da because he's got such a fine job and Mr. Lord thinks the world of him, and he's steady now and everything's going fine, and—'

'Mary Ann.' Bob was holding her hands tightly. 'Say no more. I understand, and everything is going to go as you want it with your . . . your ma and da. You take that from me.'

She stared into his face for a moment before filling her narrow chest with air, and then she smiled and said soberly, 'You won't tell me ma that I've been, will you?'

'Don't worry, Mary Ann, no one shall know about this visit, only you and me.' He touched her cheek now, saying gently, 'Don't worry your head any more, everything's going to be all right.'

There was no need to stay any longer. She rose from the chair and, picking up her basket, she made her way to the door. When Bob had opened it for her he put his hand into his inside pocket and, taking out his wallet and extracting a pound note, he handed it to her, saying, 'That's for your birthday, buy something.'

'Eeh, no! No, thank you, Mr. Quinton.'

'Go on, don't be silly.'

'But where would I say I got it?' She was staring up into his face now, wide-eyed. 'I would have to tell me ma who I'd got it from.'

The pound note fluttering in his fingers, Bob smiled wryly as he said, 'You think of everything, Mary Ann.'

Mary Ann now returned his wry smile; then after a moment of quick thinking she extended him a tentative invitation, saying, 'But if you came to my party it would be all right for me to have it then. You could just drop in as if . . . well, as if . . .'

His smile widened and his eyes twinkled as he said, 'As if I was just passing. All right, I'll accept that invitation. June the first, was it you said?'

'Well, no, it's going to be on the Saturday because we're off school then. That's a fortnight today.'

'It's a date. I'll be there and with the pound note.'

'Oh, well, it isn't just 'cos of the pound note.' She had to put that in because it was, she knew, the polite thing to say. But she added to it, 'You won't let on that I asked you?'

'Not on your life.'

She smiled her farewell now, then turned away. But she hadn't gone a few steps when she turned towards him again and said, in a low tone, 'You will go and see . . . ?'

Her voice was cut off abruptly with, 'Yes, yes, I promise you. Go on now and don't worry.' His voice pressed on her reassuringly, and she turned about and left the building site with her heart lighter than it had been for days.

Bob Quinton had hardly closed the office door on Mary Ann when another door at the other end of the room opened and Mike walked slowly into the room, and the two men stood looking across the space in silence for a moment. Then Mike, characteristically rubbing his face with the palm of his hand, muttered, 'It makes you sort of humble. My God! It isn't right for a child to have such a capacity for feeling.'

'Do you think she knew you were coming here?'

'No, no.' Mike shook his head emphatically. 'They had no idea where I was coming. Or perhaps they had their own ideas, but they would certainly not think of me coming to see you. No, things have been going over in her mind and she saw this as a solution to her own problem.'

'And to mine,' said Bob. 'But really, Mike, I didn't know where to put myself. And you behind that door and not knowing what she would come out with next. Not that there is anything in my past that you don't know. Still, that didn't make things easier. But it's odd that she should turn up at this time and you here. Isn't it? Any other time and it would have been strange enough, but at this very minute. Well' – he jerked his head – 'there are more things in heaven and earth than are dreamt of in philosophy. And now, Mike, to get back to this business.' Bob went to his desk and, lifting a blotter, took from beneath it a letter and, looking at it, he went on, 'If I follow Mary Ann's advice it will give her the lie, won't it?'

As Bob sat on the edge of the desk Mike lowered himself heavily into a chair and, nipping his lower lip between his teeth, he said, 'It's really unbelievable. Mind you, Bob, as I said, I told her to get on the bus pronto and come and tell you. But you know how you say these things and never expect a person to take you at your word. By God, she's a wicked old bitch, if ever there was one.'

'I've always known she was a trying old girl, Mike, and you may not believe it, there were times when I didn't envy you your position as son-in-law although, as you know, and you don't need me to tell you, I would gladly have been in your shoes at one time. But that's over and done with. And I always tried to be nice to the old girl because, you see, I was brought up next door and didn't want her to get the idea that because I had got on a bit it had gone to my head. Moreover, she had always liked me, and you know, say what you like, it is difficult to dislike anyone who likes you and shows it. But this' – he flicked the letter – 'that finishes me with her.'

Mike said now, 'You believe me, don't you, that I'd never clapped eyes on your wife before last Saturday morning?'

'Yes, of course I do.'

'Mind you' – Mike lowered his head now – 'I suppose I'm to blame in a way because she was so damned insistent that nobody of your wife's standard would look the side I was on, that I wanted to prove her in the wrong, but even that didn't justify her writing such a letter as that. . . . My God, I have the urge now to take the quickest transport into Shields and throttle the old bitch. . . . The trouble that old woman's caused in my life, you wouldn't believe it.'

'Oh yes I do.'

'What are you going to do about it, Bob?'

Bob looked down at the letter in his hand, which started, 'It's because I've got your interests at heart, Bob, that I'm telling you this. . . .' 'Ignore it, I think,' he said. 'It isn't written with any idea of helping me, and not wholly to get her own back on Connie for snubbing her. Its vitriolic aim is set mainly at you.'

'It's incredible, but that woman means to part Liz and me or die in the attempt. . . . Well, I swear this, if she ever managed it she wouldn't live to enjoy it.'

'I know how you feel, Mike, and I can tell you I'm not comfortable about my share in your troubles.' He gave Mike a little shame-faced look after making this statement. 'At times lately I've even thought: Without lifting a hand Mike's getting his own back.'

'No. No, man, I wouldn't want my own back on anybody. All I want to do is to carry on with my job and live in peace with Liz and the two youngsters. And for the past few years it's been like that. But as is always the case, trouble never comes alone, it has its hangers-on. I've always found that let one thing happen to me and there'll be three. And I already know what the third is to be.' He did not inform Bob of the nature of the coming trouble but he knew it would be the court case with Johnson. Instead, he added, with a grin, 'It's funny, you know, but the old devil's really done me a good turn. We've never been able to talk, us two, have we? There's always been Liz atween us.'

'Yes, I suppose you're right there, Mike, at least up until I met Connie. The odd thing is that I know Connie's right for me and me for her, yet I fight with her like I know I never would have with Lizzie.'

Mike laughed at this. 'I know what you mean there all right; it must be that fightin' and lovin' go together. Well now' – Mike straightened his back and pulled his waistcoat down – 'what are you going to do? Are you going to make it up again pronto?'

'Oh.' Bob flexed his chin and rubbed at it. 'It was me who walked out, so it's me who'll have to walk back, and that's going to take some doing. You know how it is. How does one start? And there's always the fear of a rebuff. Connie can be as aloof as an owl in a tree.'

'Aye, making it up can be a skin-stripping business. I've had some. It all depends on the time and place. It can be over in a minute or it takes days. Well now, I'll be off.' He got to his feet. 'She's had time to get the bus.'

Bob turned his head to one side and laughed. 'Mary Ann. You know, Mike, I used to envy you Mary Ann, and I still do.' He rose and walked towards the door, and as he passed Mike he said, 'That's the trouble, not having a Mary Ann of one's own.'

'Well, you can rectify that.'

'Well, we'll see.' He laughed self-consciously. 'Good-bye now, and thanks for coming, Mike. I feel better.'

'Good-bye, Bob. And let me know how things go, won't you?'

'Yes, yes, I'll do that.'

'Good-bye then.'

'Good-bye, Mike.'

'Oh.' Mike turned after taking a few steps from the door.. 'Don't forget you've got an invitation to the party.'

'Oh, the party. No, I won't forget. I'll be there, Mike.'

'Good. So long.'

'So long.'

Bob watched Mike go, liking now, with a warm understanding liking, the man he had always despised.

CHAPTER EIGHT

WHEN EXTREMES MEET

In the meantime Mary Ann had made her way to Mulhattan's Hall and Mrs. McBride's kitchen, only to find that
Mrs. McBride was out. But that didn't matter so much today
because Corny was in. He grinned at her when he opened the
door and saw her standing there, and exclaimed without any
greeting, 'Funny, I didn't see you comin'. I've just got in.
Me grannie's out, likely at the store.' Then he turned round
and walked into the room, and Mary followed him and
placed the basket on the table next to the shining cornet.

Seeing her eyes on the instrument, he exclaimed, 'Aa went
to Mr. Bradley's. By, he was good. He plays like nobody's
business. Coo! You should hear 'im. An' you know what?'
He bent slightly towards her, his eyes twinkling. 'Me grannie
was right; he is after me t' join, but for God's sake don't let
on, else she'll make it so hot for me Aa'll jump off the ferry
landin'. Aa told him Aa was a Catholic and he was decent
and said—' Now Corny broke off and, his mouth stretching
across his face, he laughed. 'You knaa what he said? He's
funny – he said it didn't matter how Aa blow meself to God
as long as Aa blows mesel there. Funny, wasn't it? Still' – his
face became serious – 'Aa'm larnin' and that's aal that
matters. It's aal to do with the breath. Look.' Before her
admiring gaze he picked up the cornet and, without making
any sound, demonstrated the art of breathing in order to play
the instrument.

'Go on, play something.' Mary Ann, seated now by the
table, looked at him in wide-eyed admiration.

'Aa dorrsn't. They' – he indicated the other dwellers in

Mulhattan's Hall by a circular movement of his head – 'they played war 'cos of the other time.'

Mary Ann knew he was referring to the morning when he had played 'He stands at the corner' and she sympathized with him by saying, 'Spoil sports.'

Corny, seating himself now at the opposite side of the table from her, suddenly changed the conversation from cornets to farming by asking abruptly, 'What've you got on yore place?'

'Got? You mean on our farm?'

'Aye.'

'Oh.' Mary Ann wriggled her bottom on the seat, and placed her elbows on the table in order to rest her face on her hands. 'Oh, we've got cows – fifteen cows and calves – seven lovely little calves – and two bulls, Bill and Neptune. Bill's nice, like a lamb.' The comparison was neither correct nor even desirable from a bull's point of view. And then, 'We've got sheep and lambs – oh, dozens of lambs, they're all over the place. And pigs – I don't like pigs, nor hens, very much. We haven't got many hens, just enough for eggs for us and Mr. Lord. And you know something?' Her head moved in the cup of her hands. 'Me da's goin' up to Scotland at the back end; he's going to buy some Galloways.'

'What d'ye want pit ponies for?'

Mary Ann gave a superior laugh. 'Galloways are not pit ponies – they're cattle, special cattle. Me da's going to start breeding them. I know it's a funny name for cattle.'

He grinned at her, then asked, 'Hev ya any horses?'

There was a pause before Mary Ann made the admission that they had no horses on the farm. Then without seemingly drawing breath she said, 'You know Sarah Flannagan, her across the road?' She swung her head up. 'Well, she's gone all hoity-toity and thinks she's the cat's pyjamas because her uncle's started a riding school near us and she can ride. And you know something?' She leant farther towards him now. 'She's after our Michael.'

'He goes to the Grammar School, disn't he?'

Corny was ignoring the main issue, and Mary Ann brought it back into focus by saying, 'She asked him to go and meet her; I heard her, I was there. She said, "Come along to our place any evening and you can help with the horses." It's only because she wants him for her lad.'

'What's yore Michael goner be?'

Mary Ann lifted her face from her hands. Corny was refusing to take the cue. As she rose from her chair she said offhandedly, 'Oh, I don't know. He'll go to college, I expect, if he passes his exams.'

Corny, too, rose, and now, picking up his cornet from the table, he looked at it as he said, 'Aa'll get on an' all. I'm goin' in a garage as soon as Aa leave school. There's piles o' money to be made oot o' cars, but Aa'm only goin' to stay there till Aa larn this properly' – he patted the cornet – 'and then Aa'll show 'em.' He turned and looked down on her now, his face solemn and plain in the extreme, and he repeated, 'Aye, Aa'll show 'em.'

'Will you tell Mrs. McBride that I've been?' Mary Ann took the things out of the basket and placed them on the table, adding, 'I'll have to be going.'

He laughed now as he looked at the eggs, butter and bacon on the table. 'Well, she won't think Mrs. Flannagan's left 'em, will she?'

They both laughed, and as he went through the door with her she inquired, 'Are you going home?'

'No. Aa'm just goin' oot for a bit.'

Mary Ann looked down at the cornet in his hand and asked, 'Well, why don't you leave that in the house?'

'Oh.' He grinned good-naturedly now. 'Me grannic's gettin' as bad as me ma; she's threatened to smash it to smithereens if she gets her hands on it. Not that she would though, mind, but Aa'm tyeking nee chances. If she comes back in a bad temper, God knaas what she'll de.'

Mary Ann smiled and nodded in sympathy, and as they went out of the house she knew that Corny was going to see her to the bus as he had done the other day, and she felt happy and sort of excited.

But the journey to the bus took much longer today than it had done previously, for they talked, and as they talked they wandered off the usual route, neither knowing who was the leader in this manoeuvre. They laughed when they finally came out at the top of Ormond Street and on to the main road, but they made no remark on the length of the detour or the long walk facing them back to the bus stop.

Mary Ann liked Corny. The more she was with him, the more she was finding that she liked to be with him. And when he suddenly asked her in his abrupt 'no nonsense' fashion whether the invitation to her party still held good, she turned on him wide astonished eyes, saying, 'Why, of course! Of course you must come, Corny,' at the same time knowing that she had missed the opportunity of following her mother's advice – express command would be a better statement – in putting Corny off. But she comforted herself with the memory of her da saying, 'You've asked him, you can't get out of it now.'

After this they walked on in a silence that lasted so long that Mary Ann, casting her eyes upwards to see how he was looking after being reassured about the invitation, experienced a most odd sensation. It wasn't weird and it wasn't frightening, but it was odd . . . lovely . . . odd. She was finding that she couldn't clearly see Corny for between them floated a silver mist that had nothing to do with the atmosphere of Jarrow. This silver mist slowly enveloped Corny. She knew he was still by her side, she knew that his suit was awful and his face wasn't much to look at, yet she knew at the same time and with a certainty that he was beautiful. The sensation was becoming more and more odd. Although the silver mist separated them, and Corny seemed to be floating away on it, she felt that he was standing close to her, very close, closer than he had stood yet, so close that she felt a heat radiating from him and into herself. It was . . . like getting into a hot bath when you are very cold. Then the mist, the beautiful silver mist, was wrenched away by no other cause than her name being spoken. But not by Corny.

Blinking as if coming out of a dream, she turned her face towards the road and the car that was pulling to a stop at the kerb. At the wheel of the car was Tony, but on the near-side, and with his face now only inches from her, was Mr. Lord.

If she had awakened in hell and been confronted by the devil she couldn't have looked more surprised.

'What is the matter with you, child? Stop blinking your eyes like that. Who is this?'

'Oh.' Mary Ann, still blinking, turned her demisted gaze now on Corny, and she gulped and said, 'He's Corny, Corny Boyle.' She gave Corny a tentative little smile as she made the introduction. Then turning her face towards Mr. Lord again, she added, 'Mrs. McBride – you know Mrs. McBride – well, she's his grandmother.'

Mr. Lord was staring past her to Corny, and Corny, with a face that could not be straighter, was returning the old man's scrutiny. And Mr. Lord, without look at Mary Ann, said, 'Get in.'

Mary Ann did not obey Mr. Lord. She didn't like the tone of his voice. She knew what it portended: a lecture. She also knew that Mr. Lord didn't like Corny, and instinct told her that she could disobey Mr. Lord without losing him, but should she reject Corny at this moment he would be gone from her forever.

'I'm going to bus it home,' she said.

Mr. Lord's eyes seemed to take a high jump from Corny to land on her, and his beetling brows drew together until they formed a bushy line across his wrinkled forehead. 'You heard what I said.' His voice was very quiet now.

'I'm—'

'Get in, Mary Ann.' It was Tony speaking; his request was calm, with no implied insult to her companion threading it, and in the moment that she hesitated before also rejecting Tony's command Corny spoke with his voice and his hand. Pushing her roughly in the back, he cried, 'Go on, get in when they tell you.' And then, lowering his head down to the window and Mr. Lord's face, he stared at the old man for a moment before declaring with deep, painful emphasis, 'Aa'm as good as you lot any day. Aye, Aa am. Aa'll show you. By God, Aa will that.'

Mary Ann shivered. Deep within her she shivered. The shiver spread to every vein of her body. She closed her eyes against it. She could have understood Corny swearing, but to take our Lord's name in vain like that, that was dreadful. It would have been dreadful if Mr. Lord hadn't heard it, but Corny had almost spat it in his face. Slowly she opened the car door, got in, and sat down. She could not bear to look at Corny; she could not bear to look at anybody; she hung her head, and when the car jerked away there was only the sound of the engine. When the silence held all the way to the farm Mary Ann realized that the situation was serious and that there would be a dust-up when she reached the house.

Mary Ann's surmise was right. Mr. Lord ordered Tony to take the main road and not turn up the hill. When Tony stopped the car outside the farmhouse Mr. Lord, getting out and ignoring Mary Ann completely, strode through the gate and up the path to the house.

Tony, turning now and leaning over the back of his seat, opened the door for Mary Ann, and as she went to get out, her head still bowed, he stopped her with his hand and, lifting her face upwards, he said softly, 'Do you like Corny?'

Near to tears and with drooping lids, she said, in an indifferent tone, 'He's all right.'

'I like him.'

Her lids came up and she stared at him as he asked, 'Where does he work?'

'He doesn't work, he's still at school.' She saw that this surprised Tony.

'He's a big fella to be still at school.'

She nodded dismally. 'That's why he's growing out of his clothes. There's a lot of them and his mother can't buy him things. He has jeans, but they look worse.'

Tony nodded without speaking for a moment, then asked, 'Where do they live? In Burton Street?'

'No, he only came there to see Mrs. McBride; he lives across the water in Howden, but I don't know where.'

Tony nodded again. Then, leaning farther towards her, he asked quietly, 'What were you talking about when we came up?'

Mary Ann blinked as she tried to remember what Corny and she had been saying before Mr. Lord barked her name, and she couldn't remember; she could only recall, and faintly now, the weird sensation about the mist, and she said to Tony, 'We weren't talking, at least I don't think we were. Why d'you want to know?'

'Oh, no reason.' Tony couldn't say that the look that the big gangling boy and the diminutive Mary Ann had been exchanging as they stood stock still on the pavement in the middle of a busy thoroughfare had even astonished him, so the effect on his grandfather must have been electric. He patted Mary Ann's head now, saying, 'Go on, face it. There'll be high jinks, but stick to your guns and no matter what he says you pick your own friends.' He emphasized this with two taps on her head as he added, 'I'm with you.'

She smiled at him sweetly now. Tony was nice; she liked Tony, oh, she did. Nearer tears than ever, she climbed out of the car and made her way to the kitchen and the battle.

'Look, Mike' — Lizzie's face was as stiff as her voice — 'she cannot bring that boy to her party.'

'Now, Liz, you look here.' Mike's tone was cool, it even suggested indifference to the seriousness of the situation. 'I don't care what the old boy said or what he didn't say, she asked him and he's comin' — that's if he wants to. But very likely after this morning's business he'll think twice about it.'

Lizzie pressed her lips together and moved her head slowly before saying, 'It's all very well you taking this "don't forget your class" stand, but who will have to bear the brunt of it? He expects you to put your foot down.' Lizzie laid emphasis on the 'you'.

'Well, let him tell me that, Liz, and I'll give him his answer.'

Lizzie stared at him. She couldn't make him out. Oh, she was fed-up, tired and weary, sick to the heart, and she asked herself why she was worrying about the outcome of Mary Ann's invitation to this lad. If Mike got it in the neck, then serve him right. Yes, serve him right. He was asking for it. He was asking for more than that. On any other occasion he would have been up in the air about the old man leading off over things that didn't concern him, over one person who didn't concern him. On other occasions he would have been shouting about his right of ownership. But since he had come in, from wherever he had been, he had looked so pleased with himself that nothing could upset him.

'Come here.' She felt herself swung round by his one big hand, but she would not look at him, and when he said softly, 'Don't you want to hear what I've got to say?' she answered tartly, 'All I want to hear is you telling her that she can't have that boy to her party.' The hand lifted from her shoulder and as it did so she chided herself, saying, 'Oh, you fool.' And when he turned from her, his voice no longer pleasant, he said, 'Well, you'll have to wait a long time afore you'll hear me tell her that, Liz, so there you have it. And don't keep on, because it won't be any use.'

When the door closed on him Lizzie turned towards her daughter who had been sitting unusually quiet in the big high-backed chair, and she cried at her, 'You're the cause of all this.'

'Oh, Ma.' It was so small as to be almost a whimper.

'The trouble you start. You never have any sense. Mr. Lord is right. Your three years at the convent might never have been; you've no idea of the fitness of things, and you nearly thirteen. And if you haven't sense now you never will have.'

Lizzie turned from the round, bright eyes, and, placing her hands on the table, she bent forward and took a number of deep breaths, and when in the next moment she felt Mary Ann's hands on her arm she shrugged them off, saying, 'Don't come near me.'

'I'll tell him, Ma. I . . . I'll tell him.'

Mary Ann's voice was breaking, but Lizzie took no notice of it, and without looking at her she said, 'The trouble's caused now; get yourself away from me.'

Mary Ann got away, she got away at a run, her hand tightly pressed over her mouth. She ran down the path into the road, hesitated for a moment and turned into the empty farmyard, her blurred vision searching wildly for some place quiet. Her eyes picked out the great barn with the steps leading to the loft. She had never been in the loft since the day she nearly fell through the trap-door into the combine harvester and her da had got hurt, so hurt. The hook on the end of his hand showed to what extent. But now at a run she made for the stairs. The door at the top was closed, indicating that no one was inside, and when she entered the dim loft and was enveloped in the sweet, dry smell of hay she gave vent to her pent-up crying. Stumbling to the farthest corner, she flung herself down on some straw behind a bale of hay and cried unrestrainedly into her arms.

She cried until she could cry no more, and then for a long time she lay shuddering at intervals.

All afternoon she lay enveloped in the dim light and the quietness. Up here the familiar farm sounds seemed a long distance away; cushioned by the bales of hay, all sound was muted. After a while she sat up, and with her back against a bale began slowly to plait some long straws. After she had made a number of plaits she then plaited them together and by the time she had finished the thick braids her fingers were moving very slowly. When as from far off she heard Len calling his particular call that brought in the cows she knew it was tea-time. But this knowledge did not arouse her hunger; she only wanted a drink.

Some time after this the light in the barn, she noticed, began to change and she thought she had better get out before it got too dark. But she didn't move; it was as if she was drugged with a mixture of the subdued light, warmth and the sweet smell that pervaded the barn. Coupled to this the feeling of exhaustion brought about by her long, violent weeping produced a form of inertia, and when she knew she was falling asleep she did nothing to try to prevent it because, as she knew, when you were asleep you didn't think about things. . . .

Some hours later Mary Ann slowly awoke from a long, deep, refreshing sleep to the sound of her mother's voice. For a moment she thought that her mother was speaking from the landing until the light flashed on to the great beams above her head, and as she dimly realized she was still in the loft she heard Lizzie's voice saying, 'It's no use looking along there, she would never come up here. She's never been near the place for years.' She did not say 'Since you lost your hand'.

As she lifted herself dazedly up on to her elbow she heard her da's heavy footsteps ringing on the boards. The light from his lantern swung over the bale and would have missed her had she not pulled herself to her feet and said dreamily, 'Da, is that you, Da?'

The next minute they were both standing in front of her, not saying a word. She blinked at them, her eyes full of sleep. She saw her ma take the lantern, then her da, stooping, hoisted her up to him with his one arm and she laid her head against his neck. And still nobody spoke.

Mike carried her down the ladder, across the yard and into the house, and even when Michael came running after them, his mouth open to ask where and when, and how, he was silenced by some sign from Lizzie.

Mike went on into the house, straight up the stairs and into her bedroom, and when he had lowered Mary Ann on to the side of the bed he stroked her head for a moment before turning away and leaving her alone with her mother. And still he hadn't spoken.

Mary Ann, coming more awake now, looked at her mother, and Lizzie, her face white and her lips trembling, put out her arms and drew her into a tight, relieved embrace, whispering as she did so, 'Oh, I'm sorry, my dear, I'm sorry.'

At this moment Mary Ann had to recall what her ma had to be sorry for, and as she remembered she said hastily, 'It's all right, Ma; it's all right.' And then, 'Don't cry, Ma . . . oh, don't cry.'

When Lizzie stopped crying and released Mary Ann she helped her to undress and seemed reluctant to leave her. As she was tucking her up in bed she said, 'Do you want a drink?'

'Please, Ma; I'm very thirsty. What time is it?'

'About half past ten.'

'Half past ten? Oh, I slept up there a long time. Did . . . did you think I was lost?'

It was some time before Lizzie answered, 'Yes . . . yes, we thought you were lost.'

'I didn't do it on purpose, Ma.'

'No, I know you didn't, my dear. Don't worry. I'll get you a drink. There now, lie down.'

Mary Ann was now wide awake, and, getting more so every moment, she waited for her mother's return. Without doing much thinking about it she knew that her ma and her were . . . kind again . . . very kind again; but she also realized that the same feeling was not in existence between her parents. It wasn't because her da hadn't spoken; she knew that was the result of him being upset because he couldn't find her, and it wasn't an angry silence. Mike, she sensed, was amenable and would make it up any time, but it was her ma who was still holding out. Mary Ann felt that she knew the reason, and as she lay looking towards the door she sensed there would never be an opportunity like the present to talk to her ma. Tomorrow her ma might still be nice to her, but tonight would be in the past, and the feelings that were high now, tomorrow they, too, would be in the past, and should she attempt to mention Mrs. Quinton's name her ma would shut her up. But tonight she held an advantage. Lizzie would not go for her tonight.

So when her mother came into the room with the drink and placed it on top of the bookcase by the head of the bed she hitched herself up into a sitting position and whispered, 'Ma, can I talk to you?'

This was the second time in one day that she had said that.

Lizzie, her back stooped, turned her face towards her daughter and said, 'It's late. And don't you want to go to sleep?'

'No, Ma, I'm not tired now. Sit down, Ma.' She pulled at Lizzie's skirt, and Lizzie sat down and Mary Ann, taking her hand and looking into her face, said, 'I want to tell you something, Ma, and I want you to promise on the Sacred Heart' – she drew the diagram of the Sacred Heart on her breast – 'not to open your mouth for . . . well, five minutes. Will you promise?'

Lizzie lowered her eyes, gave a little sigh, made the sign of the Sacred Heart on her breast and said softly, 'I promise. Go on.'

Mary Ann, too, gave a little sigh and then started quietly, but rapidly with, 'Well, Ma, it was like this. You know the Saturday I went to Beatrice's party? Well, when it was nearly over we played a game of hide-and-seek and I remembered that there were some fine big cupboards in the kitchen and when I was waiting to be found Mrs. Willoughby and Mrs. – Mrs. Quinton came into the kitchen and they began to talk.' Mary Ann's voice became slower and steadier and she tried to remember faithfully the conversation that she heard between the two women. If she embellished it here and there it only eased Lizzie's mind the more and made Mrs. Quinton out to be, as had already been stated, a nice woman. And she finished up, looking now at her mother's bowed head, 'And she's in love with him, Ma.' It was about the first time Mary Ann had used that term; she had always substituted the word 'like' for the word 'love'. 'Love' had always seemed a word belonging to the conversation of grown-ups and had a slight indecency about it, but now she said quite firmly, 'She loves him, Ma, very much, and she's lonely. And she looked lonely that time we went into Durrant's and saw her. And you see, Ma, she thinks it's you that . . . that. . . .' Mary Ann could not go on and say 'that you are the cause of her trouble'. And there was no need now, for Lizzie's hands were gripping her tightly and she saw that her ma was crying again, but it was a different kind of crying from what she had done at the kitchen table.

When Lizzie lifted her eyes to her daughter she stared at her for a moment through her blurred vision before suddenly pulling her for the second time that evening to her breast and hugging her tightly. Then she rose from the bed and, pressing Mary Ann gently back on to the pillow, she said softly, 'Go to sleep now.'

'Ma.'

'Yes, what is it?'

'You'll be all right with me da?'

Lizzie tucked the clothes round her shoulders, she straightened the covers and she stroked the tuft of hair back from Mary Ann's forehead before she said, 'Don't worry any more; everything will be all right now. God bless.' Her lips stayed longer than usual on Mary Ann's cheek and then she was gone. The door was closed, the light was out, and Mary Ann, breathing deeply, followed this by letting out a great quantity of air from her lungs before turning her head into the pillow. She was sleepy again. Everything was all right, everything – she had forgotten for the moment about Corny, Mr. Lord, the looming court case with the Johnsons and the minor trouble, but still irritating one, of their Michael and Sarah Flannagan.

CHAPTER NINE

GETTING KIND

On Sunday Mary Ann found that, contrary to what she had expected, her mother was still in the same mood in which she had been in the emotion-filled hours of the previous night – she was nice. Not that her mother was ever anything else, but her manner this morning held a special kind of niceness. Yet in spite of this she was quick to realize that things weren't back on the old footing again between her parents. Her ma, she saw, was nice to her da but it was a polite niceness. Her manner left no room for chaff or that imperative sharpness which all mothers use to keep order both with husband and children and which is recognized merely as a façade. And it was because there were none of these elements present in Lizzie's dealings with Mike and Michael and herself that Mary Ann knew that, although her mother wasn't vexed any more, she still wasn't kind with her da. Perhaps it was her da's fault and he hadn't given her the chance. Her da was like that; he'd go inside himself for days and you couldn't get near him. And yet Mary Ann had to admit to herself that he seemed pleasant enough this morning, even happy, for hadn't he walked with her to the bus when she was going to Mass and jollied her along with great lifts of his arm. And at the end of the road he had dusted her shoes with a hankie because she had got them messed up with the jumping. She would have said he was in very good fettle. And yet they weren't kind.

Everybody was nice to her all day, and Tony came to tea. It was a smashing tea. Her mother had made eight different kinds of cakes. During tea Tony asked Michael if he would like a run out in the car, and Michael, brightening visibly, answered, 'Rather', then caused a general laugh by adding, 'You know he's only asking me so's he can get past the Johnsons under escort. Once he's passed he drops me at the end of the road.'

Mary Ann kept her eyes on Tony, hoping he would include her in the invitation, and she felt slightly piqued when he didn't. He never took her out in the car, he never took her anywhere, not like he did their Michael. But later she had at least evidence that Tony thought of her and her concerns, for after he had talked quietly to her mother in the kitchen, so quietly that she couldn't hear a word, he went up to the house and returned some time later with a great parcel. And when her mother unrolled the paper and displayed to her eyes a conglomeration of clothes she asked quickly, and in surprise, 'Who's them for?'

'Who's them for?' Tony's look and voice were a laughable imitation of his grandfather, and, shaking herself, she said, 'Oh, you, Tony, you know what I mean. Who-are-they-for? There, will that suit you?'

'At least it's better. They are for your friend.'

'My friend? You mean Corny?'

'Yes, Master Corny.'

'Oh, Tony. Oh, thanks, Tony.' She grabbed his hand. Then her head on one side, she looked up at her mother and said with sudden caution, 'Isn't it nice of Tony, Ma?'

When Lizzie seemed too occupied to answer she turned to Tony again, saying, 'Oh, Corny will love them, Tony.'

'Well, I don't know.' Tony jerked his head. 'It all depends if they'll fit him – he's a great lump of a fellow. I'd like to bet that already he's got a bigger chest measurement than me. He'll be as big as you, Mike, before long.' Tony cast a laughing glance over towards Mike, where he sat smoking at the side of the fireplace, and Mike replied, 'I haven't seen the lad in years.'

'But isn't it nice of Tony, Da?' Mary Ann went and stood by the side of Mike's chair, and Mike, nodding at her, replied, 'Very nice, very nice.' But he did not sound enthusiastic and he did not look at Mary Ann as he spoke but at Lizzie's back where she was standing at the table. Then, bringing his gaze on to Mary Ann again, he stared at her before giving her an almost imperceptible nod.

Mary Ann, reading the message, turned about and went over to the table and, fingering the clothes that Lizzie was folding, asked softly, 'Can he come then, Ma?'

Lizzie went on putting the seams of a pair of trousers together and her voice was low when at last she replied, 'Well, it would be a shame to waste all these things, wouldn't it?'

Mary Ann's arms went swiftly round Lizzie's waist and she laid her head against her side for a moment. Then, lifting up a pair of almost new brown shoes from the assortment, she asked, 'When can we take them, Ma?'

'Oh, I don't know; I'd better drop Mrs. McBride a card. Corny will have to come across – the suit might need a little altering.'

Mary Ann nodded in approval. Her mother was a dab hand at altering, she had been a dab hand at trouser making – she had made Michael's for years.

Suddenly Mary Ann felt warm and happy. Everybody was nice. It was her birthday on Wednesday, but the great day would be Saturday when she had her party. And Corny could come. For some reason she couldn't fathom, Corny's presence at her party promised it an aura of glamour, which quality had not been suggested by the persons of any of her posh friends, male or female. It was a very odd situation, which, although she did not know it, had to do with natural, very natural in her case, selection.

Mary Ann retained the nice feeling until Monday morning, when, sitting at breakfast, she watched Mike open another sealed letter. It was a longish envelope and the paper was thick and stiff and she felt a fleeting return of anxiety as she watched him reading it. But the anxiety fled when he did not place it in his pocket but, putting it on the table, laid his hand flat on it and stared down at it as he asked grimly, 'Who do they think they're trying to frighten?'

'What is it?' The apprehension Lizzie was feeling came over in her voice and Mike answered without looking at her, 'A solicitor's letter.'

'Let me see it here.' Lizzie held out her hand, and Mike, after a moment, passed her the letter.

The letter was headed: Ringmore Chambers, Purley Street, Newcastle-on-Tyne, and at the left side were the names Bristow, Yates and MacFarlace, Solicitors, and the letter began:

Dear Sir,

Our Client, Mr. Henry Johnson of Moor Farm, has acquainted us with the events which took place at Moor Farm, Fellhurst, on Saturday, May 20th.

We are instructed that at that time and place you seriously assaulted our Client, knocking him to the ground and occasioning him to sustain a broken ankle in addition to bruisings and shock, as a result of which he has had to seek and receive medical attention.

We are writing, therefore, on his behalf to inform you that he proposes to seek redress in the courts for what has occurred.

It is not possible for us at this stage accurately to quantify his claim until it is seen how he recovers from the injuries which he sustained and whether or not there is likely to be any permanent disability, and it therefore will be a little time before the proceedings which we have instructions to commence are served upon you.

In the meantime if you have any proposals to make concerning the matter you may care to communicate with us, and if you wish to take legal advice before doing so no doubt you will do so.

Yours faithfully,
Charles Bristow

Mary Ann watched her mother put the letter slowly down on the table and, almost as if she was copying Mike's attitude, lay her hand on it and with a notable tremor in her voice ask, 'What will be the outcome of it?'

Mike did not answer for a moment but rose from the table and, going to the mantelpiece, he took his pipe from the rack and prepared to fill it. Not until it was almost full did he speak. 'They'll take me to court,' he said. 'And if I lose the case I'll have to stump up, that's all.'

He came to the table, picked up the letter, then took his coat from the head of the couch, but before making his way to the door he paused for a moment by Lizzie's chair and said quietly, 'Don't worry, things'll pan out.'

Mary Ann watched them looking at each other. It seemed as if they looked at each other for a long time before her mother's eyes dropped away and her da left the kitchen.

'If he loses, how much would they make him pay?' Michael was looking earnestly at Lizzie, who, rising from the table now, said, 'Oh, I don't know. Anyway, why should he lose? He's got a good case. Come along, get ready for school.'

Michael did not pursue the subject as Mary Ann would have done, but in his thoughtful, serious way he got his things together and after saying good-bye to Lizzie left the house.

Mary Ann hadn't to leave for another fifteen minutes and she made up her mind to go and find her da – he hadn't said good-bye to her. But she was forestalled in this by Lizzie saying, 'You've got time to run up with these eggs to Ben. They've never had any since Friday, they must be out.'

Mary Ann made no protest, she might see her da on the way. She followed her mother into the stone larder and took the wire basket in which lay a dozen eggs, and, hurrying almost at a run but carefully so she wouldn't trip, she went up the hill, through the side gate, round the courtyard and towards the back door. But long before she reached the door she heard Mr. Lord's voice, and she knew he was going at it, and likely at Tony. Her last surmise was confirmed when, with finger on the bell, she was about to press it – she never dared to enter Ben's kitchen without permission; she could walk straight into the drawing-room through the french windows, but never into the kitchen – when the door was wrenched open and Tony marched past her, only to draw up quickly and turn an anger-suffused face towards her.

Looking at him in amazement, she saw that he was right mad about something, and then she sensed that the anger in his look seemed to be directed towards her, and there was not only anger in the look. What it was she couldn't put a name to, but she found she wanted to turn her face away from it, it was as if Tony hated her. But she had done nothing, nothing at all. After a swift searching of her mind and finding her conscience clear over the last few hours she went to speak about a quite irrelevant matter, the eggs. Her mouth open and the wire basket held up, she was about to draw his attention to them when he swung away from her and strode towards the gate.

What was up with him? He needn't take it out on her because Mr. Lord had gone for him.

'Give them here.'

She turned to find Ben's hand extended towards her, and was further amazed to find that his expression bore some resemblance to Tony's. When he grabbed the basket from her she curbed her natural reaction to demand, 'What's up with you all?' and asked, 'Can I have the cage back?' and her face stretched in indignation when she heard his reply.

'You should be in a cage, along with the rest of them. . . . All women should be in cages.'

She watched the old man shamble into his kitchen. What was the matter wih him, saying she should be in a cage? Ben and her were usually all right; he was nicer to her than he was to anybody on the farm. Of course that wasn't saying much, not for Ben. But still, to say that she should be in a cage . . .

When he returned with the empty basket she demanded stoutly, 'What's up? I haven't done anything.'

'You'll be doin' things till the day you die. Go on. Go on now.' He flung his arm widely over her head.

And Mary Ann went. She went backwards for a number of steps, for her amazement was unbounded. She hadn't done anything, she knew she hadn't done anything, and she told herself all the way down the hill that she hadn't done anything. She was so disturbed she even forgot to look for her da.

When she reached the kitchen she said to her mother, 'Has Tony been in, Ma?'

'No.' Lizzie turned her head and looked at Mary Ann, her

eyes narrower as she asked, 'Why, what's the matter? Why are you looking like that?'

'I don't know, Ma.' And she didn't know. 'They were going at it up there, Mr. Lord and Tony, and Tony passed me without speaking. And then Ben went for me. I've done nothing, have I, Ma?'

Lizzie stared at her daughter and then she asked softly, 'Well, only you know that. Have you?'

'No, Ma, honest. Look, on the Sacred Heart.' She made the sign on her chest again. 'I swear, Ma. Well, I've never been out, have I?'

'No. No, you haven't, not since tea-time yesterday, any-way.' Lizzie stood thoughtful for a moment and then said briskly, 'Well, if you haven't done anything there's nothing to worry about. Go along and get your coat on and get off.'

A few minutes later Mary Ann left the house and she turned into the farmyard determined to say good-bye to her da and, incidentally, to see if he could throw any light on the matter of Tony. But this solace was denied her, for on nearing the office she heard Mr. Lord's voice. He was talking to her da and what amazed her now still further was that he wasn't shouting, his voice was quiet. Although she couldn't catch what he was saying, she seemed to detect a sympathetic note in it which was even more puzzling still.

But as nothing would induce her to face Mr. Lord this morning, even in spite of his quiet-sounding tone, she turned about and made her way to the bus and school. It was Monday again and the pattern of the week was set . . . at least for her.

The day seemed interminable to Mary Ann, although during break and lunch hour she was hovered over and made much of by her two friends who wanted to talk of nothing but the party and those who were likely to be present – Roy Connor for instance and Alec Moore. Oh, Alec Moore was the tops. Janice hugged herself at the mere mention of Alec Moore.

Mary Ann simulated interest; she did her best because a certain standard of enthusiasm was expected of her, but all the time her mind was back at the farm and the incident of this morning.

For a short space Beatrice did catch her attention; it was when she said that her Aunt Connie had been inquiring after her.

Mary Ann had thought quite a bit on and off about Mr. Quinton since Saturday, and she had come to the conclusion that if his coming to her party only resulted in her being able to accept the pound note, then somehow his visit would be wasted. To settle this matter once and for all, Mrs. Quinton should be there. But she didn't know where Mrs. Quinton lived and she was averse, somehow, to asking Beatrice for this information, and should she tell her to bring her Aunt Connie to the party Beatrice would laugh. Aunt Connie was all right, but she was grown-up and Beatrice had voiced the opinion more than once that all grown-ups were stuffy. Mary Ann had always agreed with her, so you could hardly ask anybody who was stuffy to a party. Yet unless she came and ... got kind with Mr. Quinton, things in a way would remain as they were, and Mr. Quinton at large without a wife was, even after the reassurance of Saturday morning, still a potential danger to her da.

It was a chance remark of Beatrice's that gave Mary Ann the solution. 'I was on the phone to Aunt Connie on Saturday night,' she said, 'and it was then she asked about you.' If Beatrice could phone her Aunt Connie, why shouldn't she? The only snag was she had never used a phone in her life. There was one in her da's office, and when occasionally she would put her hand on it her da would say, 'Now, now, leave that alone', as if it was alive and would bite. But now the time had come, she told herself, when she must try it.

This matter settled as far as she could take it at the moment, her mind returned to the farm again and the question, What had happened up at the house this morning? And when school was over and the usual gushing farewells exchanged she couldn't get home quickly enough to ascertain if her ma had found out anything.

Apparently Lizzie was no wiser than when Mary Ann had left her, for to her immediate inquiry, 'Have you seen anybody?' Lizzie replied, 'No, not a soul today. Only your da, of course.'

Mary Ann looked at her mother and was able to see right away that things between her ma and da were also as she'd left them this morning. They hadn't made it up.

It was Michael who brought Tony's name up at tea-time, saying, 'What's the matter with Tony?' He looked towards Mike as he spoke. 'He went along the road in the car as if the devil was after him.'

'Didn't he stop?' asked Lizzie.

'Well, he didn't actually pass me; I saw him turning up the lane. He took the hill as if he was in the races.'

When Michael's gaze turned slowly on to his sister and he asked gruffly, 'Have you been up to something?' she flared round on him. That was after banging her cup on to her saucer and gulping a mouthful of tea. 'No, I haven't, our Michael. Why should I get the blame for everything?'

'Now, now, that's enough of that.'

'Well, Ma, he blames me for everything.'

Michael turned again to his father. 'Do you know what's up with him, Da?'

Mike's eyebrows went up and his gaze went down and, shaking his head, he said slowly, 'No, I don't; I'm in the dark as much as you. I've never clapped eyes on him the day and that's unusual. I don't think that's happened all the time he's been here except when he was on holiday. But the night's young, he'll likely look in later.'

But Tony did not look in later. And when it was time for bed and Mike had locked up for the night he stood in the middle of the kitchen winding his watch, and after a time, during which he contemplated the banked-down fire, he remarked, 'There's something fishy about this. I don't like it.'

'Do you think it's to do with Lorna Johnson?'

'I just don't know, I haven't a clue.'

'Did he . . . Mr. Lord say anything?'

'Not about Tony, but he was as smooth as butter with me. I always feel he's up to somethin' when he's smooth. When I showed him that letter this mornin' he said, "Oh, not to worry." He says he knows Bristow personally and will have a talk with him; the matter might be dealt with out of court ... for a stated amount. He seemed sure that I'd lose the case if it came up, and if I let it go on I'll be up to my neck, he says. He's very likely right an' all. Hell!' Mike abruptly walked towards the fireplace now and, putting his foot on the fender and gripping the rod under the mantelpiece, went on grimly, 'I hate to think of Johnson getting a penny of mine. I've never saved in me life until now and it's to go on him. My God!'

'Mike.' Lizzie's voice came from close behind him and he turned slowly and confronted her. 'I've got a little put by. I saved it out of the housekeeping and the presents you give me. It's about thirty pounds. You know it's there for you if you want it.'

After a short while, during which they gazed fixedly at each other, Mike exclaimed thickly, 'Liz.' His arm came out and around her neck and pulled her close to him. When her face was hidden from him he put his mouth into her hair and muttered, 'I don't care a damn really about Johnson, or his courts, or the old boy. It's us. Let's talk this out, Liz ... now, for I can't stand much more of that angelic acceptance of yours, it wears me down. You think I went off on a personal spree on Saturday, don't you ... that's what's worrying you, isn't it?'

When Lizzie's head moved against him but she made no comment, he said, 'Look at me,' and when he had pulled her face level with his she felt a stab of pain go through her as he said, 'I don't want to tell you this at all because it's going to hurt,' but when he added, 'but not so much as if I'd gone off to meet Mrs. Connie Quinton,' the pain subsided and her lips parted questioningly. 'But I went to see a Quinton all right – Bob.'

'Bob! You went to see Bob on Saturday?' Lizzie's face was screwed up now.

'Aye, I did. That letter I got was from him. Your mother had written to him about ... about his wife and me. ... There now, there, don't look like that; I told you it wouldn't be pleasant.'

'Oh, Mike!'

'Don't worry, Liz; she's done her worst and failed. It didn't upset me; nothing really upsets me but you and me not being at one.'

'Oh, Mike!' Lizzie seemed incapable of saying anything else at the moment. She was really horrified that once again her mother had tried to harm this man, and she closed her eyes and bent her head into Mike's neck as he said, 'She did me a good turn in a way; I never thought I'd get on with Bob Quinton, but I'd like to bet we're friends for life now. And I've got another little surprise for you. You'd better sit down.' He led her to the couch, and when they were seated he looked at her with a wry smile on his face as he said, 'Bob had another visitor the time I was there – your daughter.'

'Mary Ann!'

'Aye, Mary Ann. None other. I skedaddled into the lavatory when I saw her coming.'

'What on earth was she doing there? Was it at his house?'

'No, in the works' office. She told him she'd been hiding in a cupboard at that party the other Saturday and overhead Connie and her cousin talking about you.'

'Oh no, not that.' Lizzie put her hand over her mouth.

'Did you know about the cupboard episode, Liz?'

'Yes' – Lizzie's voice was just a whisper – 'she told me on Saturday night. She tried to tell me before but I wouldn't listen to her. Oh, my goodness, what does he think?'

Mike's eyes were soft now as he looked at Lizzie and said quietly, 'He'll think just what she told him, that his wife loves him. Yes, she told him that, and also that her ma loves her da and thinks the world of him ... oh, the world of him.' There was a tremor of laughter in Mike's voice now.

'Oh, Mike!' Although the tears were gushing from Lizzie's eyes her lips were smiling. 'She's right, she's right.'

They were locked hard together and Mike's kiss had been long on her lips when his glance was drawn upwards and towards the door leading into the hall, there to see Mary Ann standing in her nightgown. Slowly he withdrew his mouth from Lizzie's and, pressing her arm tight as a warning, said as casually as he could, 'Come in. What are you up for at this hour?'

With slow, measured steps Mary Ann came into the kitchen and looked at her mother. Lizzie was not looking at her daughter, but was busily straightening her hair, and when she went to rise from the couch Mike's hand prevented her, and he spoke again to his daughter, saying, 'Come here.'

Mary Ann now went and stood before them and she looked from one to the other, blinking her eyes rapidly the while. It did not and never had embarrassed her to see her parents loving; rather she was filled with the joy that came to her at only rare times, like the morning she was dancing with the lambs or when in some stage of benediction she would be carried away out of herself.

She fell against them now, her arms around their necks, bringing their three heads together, and she started to laugh. And Mike laughed, and Lizzie laughed, and for a space this large section of Mary Ann's world became wonderful.

CHAPTER TEN

NEVER JUDGE A MAN BY THE FIT
OF HIS CLOTHES

HER ma and da were kind again. Except for the court
business and Tony's oddness, most of the sky was rosy. It
only required that Mr. Quinton should meet Mrs. Quinton
and everything would be fine. She pulled open the heavy
door of the telephone kiosk.

When some seconds later it swung heavily to behind her
she wondered for a moment if she'd ever have the strength to
open it again – well, somebody would be sure to come along
and help her. Gingerly she put down her school satchel on
the cleanest part of the floor, then reached up for the top-
most of the three great books.

From tacit inquiries of Beatrice and Janice she had learned
that you had only to look in the telephone directory and
there was the name and number of everybody in Newcastle.
It had sounded so easy. She looked and looked, but she
realized there were three people standing in a row outside
the kiosk and they were all looking at her. They were two
women and a man, and as she returned their gaze the man
pulled the door open and asked, 'Can I help you, hinnie?'

'I'm looking for Newcastle.'

He looked down at the book. 'Well, you won't find it in
that one; here's the one you want.' He reached in and pulled
the bottom book forward. 'Who do you want in Newcastle?'

She looked at him for a moment before saying, 'Quinton.
The name's Quinton.'

'What's the initial?'

'What? Oh, you mean his . . . Mr. Quinton's?'

'Well, whoever pays for the phone.' He laughed, and the women joined in, and she said, 'His name's Bob . . . Robert.'

'Robert . . . R. Quinton.' He thumbed down the page, then asked, 'R. J. Quinton, Burley House, Thyme Crescent, is that it?'

'I think so.'

The man and she stared at each other, and then he said, 'You just think so, you're not sure?'

When she didn't answer he added, 'Well, the number's Newcastle 4343601. Can you think of that, or will I get it?'

When she still did not answer, the man picked up the phone and got the exchange and stood with the receiver to his ear and his eyes fixed quizzically on her. He stood for some time in this attitude, and just as his eyes jerked towards the mouthpiece Mary Ann put in hastily, 'I want Mrs. Quinton, Mrs. Connie Quinton.'

'Oh, aye. . . . Hullo there, is that Mrs. Quinton, Mrs. Connie Quinton?'

Mary Ann watched him listening, she watched him nod his head. Then passing the instrument down to her he said, 'There you are, go ahead.'

But she did not immediately go ahead, she did not go ahead until the man, with a laugh and some remark to the women, left the box and closed the door behind him. And then she said:

'Hallo.'

The voice that came to her over the wire didn't sound like Mrs. Quinton's but she knew that it was, and when the voice said, 'Who is it?' she replied immediately, 'Mary Ann . . . Mary Ann Shaughnessy.'

'Oh . . . Mary Ann!' The voice sounded high and surprised. And then it said, 'How are you, Mary Ann?'

'Very well, thank you.'

'And your mother and father?'

'They're all right.' She was stumped for a moment. How did you talk to somebody when you weren't looking at them? It was an experience new to her. Then the voice over the wire helped her out. After a pause it said, 'Were you wanting to tell me something, Mary Ann?'

'No, no, I was only going to ask you if you'd come to my party . . . my birthday party, on Saturday, about four o'clock.'

There followed another pause, so long that she held the receiver farther away from her for a moment and looked at it, then stuck it quickly back against her ear again as the voice said, 'I would love that, Mary Ann. Thank you very much for asking me. Beatrice and Janice are coming, aren't they? I'll run them over.'

'No, no, don't do that. Well, what I mean is, I haven't told Beatrice I was asking you. Could you not . . . well, could you not just make it that you were popping in?'

Another pause, even longer this time, then the voice said, 'Does your mother know that you have asked me to your party, Mary Ann?'

There was no time to think about lying and the consequences of lying, for she knew instinctively that if her mother was not supposed to be in on this invitation Mrs. Quinton wouldn't just drop in, although her da had invited her, so she said hastily, 'Yes. Yes, she does, but I wanted to ask you. I wanted to . . . to phone.' And then to give a valid reason for the way the invitation was being given she said, 'I've never phoned before. This is the first time and I wanted to do it. And I never told Beatrice because it's a girls' party and she'd . . . she'd . . .'

She heard Mrs. Quinton laugh gently before saying, 'All right, Mary Ann; it'll be as you wish – I'll just drop in.'

'Thank you, Mrs. Quinton, thank you. Good-bye.'

'Good-bye, Mary Ann. Good-bye.'

Mary Ann heard a click on the wire and she took the receiver away from her ear and again looked at it. It was difficult to know how Mrs. Quinton felt when she couldn't see her face – her voice had sounded a bit odd when she had said, 'Good-bye, Mary Ann.'

'Well, you've got it over?' The man had pulled open the door, and she turned to him and said, 'Will I put it back now?'

'Yes, that's the procedure, put it back.'

She put the receiver back on the stand, and as she went from the box the man and the two women laughed, which caused her to feel slightly indignant – she could see nothing funny in phoning. Anyway, she had done it, and she had also done her best to put things right between the Quintons. She could do no more. Only it was a long time till Saturday to see the results of her strategy.

On Wednesday morning everybody was jolly at breakfast; at one point even Lizzie was rolling helplessly with her laughter. This was when Mary Ann, her face straight but her eyes wide with suppressed merriment, read aloud a card, the blood-connection duty card which she received each year from Mrs. McMullen. And this one, under the circumstances even more farcical than previous ones, read:

TO MY DEAREST GRANDDAUGHTER

The sweetest day in all the year
Is when I send you this.
May all your life be free from care
And overflowing with bliss.
>From
Your Grandmother

'Oh!' said Mike, wiping his eyes. 'Thank God we can see the funny side of it.'

But now Lizzie said nothing, until Michael, saying as if to himself, 'The sweetest day in all the year,' caused a fresh outbreak of laughter, when she cried, 'Enough! enough! Come on, get your breakfasts, you'll all be late.'

It was a pity, Mary Ann thought, that she had to go to school on her birthday. She would like to have browsed over her cards, of which she had fifteen, and try on the dress her mother had bought her. Then there was the lovely encyclopaedia from her da to be perused, not forgetting the book from Michael by Nancy Martin called *Young Farmers in Scotland*. She was even generous enough on this particular morning not to question his choice, for he had also bought her a brooch with her birthday stone in it. Oh yes, everything was wonderful, even if she did have to scatter to school.

But as she finished golloping her breakfast she did remark to herself with a note of regret that no one had brought up the matter of the riding lessons. Well, she didn't want to go, anyway. Not where Sarah Flannagan was, that she didn't.

Then into the joy of the morning intruded another thought, and she knew she was not alone with this particular thought, for although neither her ma and da nor their Michael had mentioned Tony they were all thinking about him – he hadn't been near the house since Sunday. She knew also that they had thought, as she had, that her birthday would bring him in. Last year he hadn't waited until breakfast but had come diving upstairs before she was up. He had given her a lovely present of a camera and a box of candies. She had the box yet and it still had the big bow on it.

She couldn't see why a row with Mr. Lord should prevent him from coming in. He'd had rows before and far from keeping him away they had kept him longer in the kitchen talking. Her da, she knew, was getting a bit worried about the business. He had said last night that short of waylaying him and asking him outright it looked as if they'd remain in the dark. But the job was how to waylay him, for he hadn't clapped eyes on him. And then he had turned to her and asked quietly, 'Sure you haven't been up to anything?' And she had vowed as she made the sign of the Sacred Heart, 'No, Da. On the Sacred Heart, no.'

The arrangements for the day were set by a card to Lizzie from Mrs. McBride, which said she would have Corny at Mulhattan's Hall that evening at five o'clock and Lizzie knew she would always be more than pleased to see her. And so it was arranged that Mary Ann, who did not want to miss the look of wonder on Corny's face when he received this bundle of fine clothes, would go straight to Burton Street from school and meet up with her mother.

A meeting with Mrs. McBride and Corny in the middle of the week she looked upon as an unexpected treat, and its anticipation coloured her birthday to a rosy glow. At ten minutes to five she jumped off the bus and made her way hastily to Burton Street.

She couldn't explain the feeling to herself other than that

she seemed to become different when she was in this part of the town. People spoke to her. They hailed her: 'Hullo there, Mary Ann!' 'How you doing, Mary Ann?' 'How's yer da, Mary Ann?' 'By! Mary Ann, yer lookin' grand.' She always felt as if she was somebody when she came to Burton Street.

Wanting to get there quickly, she took a short cut and was turning the corner round by Tullis's, the outdoor beer shop, when she bumped slap into Mrs. Flannagan. She had said, 'Pardon. Oh, I'm sorry!' before looking up into the thin, peevish face of Mrs. McBride's – and her own – enemy.

She drew back from the contact as if she had been stung by an enormous wasp. Then her face showed blank amazement as Mrs. Flannagan spoke. It was as if the wasp by a magic touch had turned into a harmless bumble-bee, for Mrs. Flannagan was smiling her thin smile, and it was very hard to believe that in her refeened voice which Mary Ann knew she kept for special occasions she was speaking to her. 'Oh, it's you, Mary Ann. And how are you?'

Mary Ann backed into the gutter, making a wide circle around this alarming Mrs. Flannagan, and she mumbled as she did so, 'All right, thank you.'

'And how is everyone?'

Everyone meant her ma and da. Mrs. Flannagan was asking after her ma and da! She gulped, and still retreating backwards she said again, 'All right, thank you.'

'That's right. That's right.'

What was right Mary Ann couldn't make out, but she nodded before turning swiftly about and making for Mrs. McBride's.

Mrs. Flannagan had spoken to her . . . civilly. The world would surely come to an end. And then she began to giggle inside, seeing a picture of herself when she got home mimicking Mrs. Flannagan to her da. And she would tell Mrs. McBride. Yes, she would make her ma and Mrs. McBride split their sides telling them how Mrs. Flannagan had spoken to her. 'And how is everyone?'

She ran the rest of the way up the street to Mulhattan's Hall. But when she reached the steps her run dropped to a walk, and then she stopped. Mrs. McBride was leading off, she was leading off something awful. For a moment she thought her ma had not arrived. But it was Lizzie, wearing her keep-your-tongue-quiet look, who opened the door to her.

When she entered the room there was Mrs. McBride standing at one side of the table, her fists dug into her great hips, and at the other side stood Corny, a plain, furious-faced Corny, and between them, on the table, were the clothes her ma had brought – the suit, the shoes, the two shirts, the pullover, the socks, and the three ties. That the matter was serious Mary Ann knew immediately, for Mrs. McBride did not turn to welcome her but went on yelling at her grandson.

'Who the hell d'you think you are to turn your nose up at things like this!' Mrs. McBride's fist came off her hip and she lifted a shirt high in the air with a flick of her finger. 'Stuff you'll never be able to afford in all your born days, for you'll end up playing that blasted cornet in the back streets. That'll be your end, me lad. You'll take those things and you'll say thank you very much and you'll put them on. Aye, you'll put them on if I have to strip you and dress you meself.'

'Aa won't . . . Aa won't hev 'em. Aa've towld ye, Gran.' Corny's voice was not loud, and because it was not loud it carried more weight and power than his Grannie's. 'Aa din't want his things. If me ma can't buy me new clothes Aa've towld ya Aa'll wait till Aa can buy 'em mesel'. But Aa divn't want them!' He flicked his hand across the table as if swiping away something repulsive.

'In the name of God!' Fanny closed her eyes for a moment before opening them wide again and turning them on Lizzie. And now her voice was a tone lower as she said, 'Lizzie, would you believe it if you weren't seeing with your own eyes and hearing with your own ears? Would you believe it? Here's this walking scarecrow—' Fanny now flung her head round towards Corny. '—that's all you are, a walking scarecrow, a laughing-stock, a big gowk. You're fond of singing "He stands at the corner and whistles me out, With his hands in his pockets and his shirt hanging out", but that's a respectable figure compared with you, for you're hanging out from all points, north, south, east, and west. Your arms are hanging out of your coat, your legs are hanging out of your trousers, and your neck's craning a mile up out of your shirt. Have you seen yerself lately?'

'Aye. And them that doesn't like me they knaa what they can dee. An' ye can taalk yerself sky-blue-pink, Gran, but Aa'm not takin' that aald bloke's things.'

'They're not Mr. Lord's things, Corny.' Lizzie's voice was soothing. 'They belong to Tony. He's the young fellow, and very nice, you would like—'

'Aye, Aa've seen him. He was in the car the other day. Aa divn't want his things.' Corny's voice was getting lower now and quieter, and his head drooped as he added, 'Thanks, aall the same, Mrs. Shaughnessy, but ye see, Aa divn't want them things.'

'All right, Corny, I under—'

'Well now, you don't want them things?' Fanny had started again. 'Well now, listen to me, me lad, and I'm tellin' you: this is an ultimatum as good as ever you'll hear comin' over the wireless. I said an ultimatum, and that's what I mean. You take them things and you wear them or else you never put your nose in this door again.'

Corny raised his head and looked at his grannie, and his grannie looked at him. They stood thus for a long time, or so it seemed to Mary Ann, an unbearably long time, and she felt an awful ache pass through her chest when Corny, still looking at his grannie, said simply, 'Fair enough, Gran, fair enough.'

Mary Ann's eyes, wide with apprehension, followed him as he walked round the table, past his grannie, past her ma and out of the door. They were letting him go.

She looked swiftly to where Mrs. McBride stood, her arms akimbo once again, her face purple hued, and from there to her mother, who looked terribly troubled. Then without a word to either of them she turned swiftly about and ran out of the room.

When she reached the bottom of the steps Corny was half-way down the street. She scampered after him and, pulling up breathlessly by his side, exclaimed, 'Oh, Corny! Oh, you didn't mean that, did you?'

Corny did not answer. He was striding along, his arms moving as if he was on a route march.

Mary Ann tried again. Walking and running alternately, she looked up at him and said, 'You'll have to go and see her . . . your grannie. She's in a bad temper, that's why she said you hadn't to go back. Will you go and see her? Will you, Corny?'

When there was still no answer to her plea, she said with a touch of indignation, 'Everybody was doing everything for the best, and, as Mrs. McBride said, they were lovely clothes, and it will be a long time before you can buy things like them, and—'

He had stopped so abruptly that she went on for a few steps before she realized he had come to a halt. When she went back to him he looked down on her and with his mouth grim, yet trembling slightly, he said, 'Then if Aa can't buy 'em Aa'll hev to dee withoot, won't Aa? An' that's just what Aa'll dee. An' Aa'll tell ya somethin' else when Aa'm on. She didn't want me to hev 'em no more'n Aa did mesel.'

'What! Your grannie?'

'Aye, me grannie. That was aall a put-on show cos she didn't want to upset yer ma. Aa knaa, Aa knaa me grannie, Aa knaa her inside oot. An' Aa knaa she knaas how Aa felt, for aall her life she's never had nowt else but second-hand, aye, an' third-hand things. Me ma says she's never had a new rag since the day she was born. . . . Well, that's not gonna happen to me. If Aa can't buy 'em new, then Aa'll dee withoot. Ye can tell that to yer Mister God-Almighty. Ye can an' aall.'

As Mary Ann stared up into the tight, angry face she wanted to cry. She wanted to cry for Mrs. McBride, who had never had a new thing in her life; she wanted to cry for Corny, who was determined not to start on the same road. She wanted to cry because of the feeling she had for Corny. It wasn't like the feeling she had had the other day, all vague and misty, it was a firm feeling, solid, and it was taking up a large space dead-centre of her chest, and it made her say very quietly, 'Well, I don't care what you wear.'

Corny stared at her for some time before swinging away and saying, 'Aw! Go on back home.'

But Mary Ann didn't go back home, she continued to walk by Corny's side in the direction of the ferry. It was she who was setting him home now. It was a silent journey until just before they came to the ferry landing, when Corny, looking straight ahead and as if he was continuing the conversation said, 'Ye divn't mind round here, round these quarters, but ye'd soon turn yer nose up if Aa showed up at your place like this.'

'I wouldn't. No, I wouldn't.'

'Aw well, yer needn't worry.' He moved his head in a flinging motion from side to side.

'I'm not worrying at all. But I wouldn't mind, I wouldn't.' She felt that she had to convince him that she wouldn't mind, yet somewhere in the back regions of her head she knew that she would mind. Not for herself – if there was only to be Corny and herself she wouldn't mind – but she would mind others seeing him.

The first time she had walked in the street with him she knew she was ashamed of people seeing him with her, but now she was only ashamed of people seeing him so poorly put on.

'Ye can't come any farther.'

She realized this, as they had reached the ticket office, and she looked up at him sadly, waiting for him to say something. But all he said was a muttered, 'So long.' Yet the quiet, subdued tone told her that in a way he was thanking her for her championship.

When he got his ticket and moved away from the box-office without again looking at her, she cried after him loudly, 'Corny! I'll . . . I'll expect you on Sunday.'

Corny did not pause in his walk, he went on towards the ferry where it was waiting to cross the Tyne, and the waters of the river were not so deep and wide as the gulf between them. Mary Ann became acutely aware of this as she watched his gangling figure disappear, and for a moment she hated the circumstances that separated them. She wished, oh, she wished with a deep longing, that she lived once again in the attic in Mulhattan's Hall, and then it wouldn't have mattered what Corny wore, she could have talked to him every day in the streets and nobody would have raised an eyebrow.

When she could no longer see him she turned away and walked slowly back to Burton Street. She was sad with a new kind of sadness. It was a different sadness to that which she experienced when her ma and da weren't all right; this sadness was a more private feeling, she couldn't work it out with herself. She did not know that she was paying the first instalment on the price that is attached to rising socially. Not only were you expected to say mother and father instead of ma and da. Not only were you expected to speak grammatically in everything you said. Not only were you expected to say you were going to the bathroom when you were really going to the lavatory. But there were the big issues, like forgetting the people you once knew just because they dressed differently and talked differently. Dimly Mary Ann became aware that of all the things entailed by a rise in position the one that concerned people affected her most, and in the depth of her subconscious, unknown to herself, a revolt began, a revolt against everything and everybody who would try to turn her from . . . her ain folk.

CHAPTER ELEVEN

THE NIGHT BEFORE THE PARTY

It had been a hectic week for Lizzie. Cleaning and polishing from the top to the bottom of the house and baking in preparation for the great day, her hands and feet had been busy from morning until night. Her mind, too, had been busy, and it was not completely at rest.

Mike and she were all right again – she thanked God for that, oh she did – but there had been the rather distressing business of Corny and the clothes on Wednesday which had upset her more than a little. She had felt ashamed of her attitude towards the boy, yet at the same time being glad that he wouldn't be turning up at the party, with or without the clothes. He was over-big and too near to being what Lizzie considered a youth for Mary Ann to shower her first outgoing affection on; besides, he was a rough kind of lad. Yet in spite of all this, some part of Lizzie's heart was drawn to the boy, for she recognized in him traits that were in Mike, pride and stubbornness, and she had thought that he could be her son more than Michael was. Then, too, there was the business of the looming court case. Like Mike she was sick at heart to think that their little bit of savings might have to go to people like the Johnsons. And last, but certainly not least, was the business of Tony. She just could not understand Tony. And as she stood at the table filling the boat-shaped tins with spoonfuls of cake mixture, she brought the subject up again with Mike.

Mary Ann, almost sick with excitement – at least Lizzie imagined it was excitement that had caused the tummy upset – was in bed and asleep, and Michael was in the front room doing his homework. They had the kitchen to themselves. Pausing with the spoon in her hand, Lizzie looked at Mike, where he sat by the fire reading a farming journal, and asked, 'Haven't you any idea at all about Tony?'

'No. . . . No,' said Mike again. But he did not lift his eyes from the magazine as he spoke. Most of the day a thought had troubled Mike, and he said to himself again now, 'Oh, away, he would have more sense than to take umbrage at that.'

'Well, I think his attitude is very odd and I think, Mike, it's your business to find out what the trouble is.'

'Hold your hand a minute, Liz. Who am I to go barging up to him and ask why he hasn't been in? The door's open for him; if he doesn't want to come in that's his business.'

As Lizzie was about to make further comment Mike held up his hand and said, 'Sh! Somebody's coming up the yard.'

'Good gracious!' Lizzie had leaned towards the window, and now, turning her head swiftly, she whispered, 'It's Ben.'

'Ben?' Mike was on his feet. Ben had never been to the farm-house door since they came here. Ben's world centred around the house on the hill and its master. Mike went quickly to the back door and a few minutes later he re-entered the kitchen with Ben at his side.

Looking kindly at the old man and trying to hide the surprise she felt at his visit, Lizzie said, 'Come away in, Ben. It is nice to see you.'

'Surprised?' Ben's voice held its usual gruff note.

Before Lizzie could attempt to lie pleasantly Mike said, 'Here, take a seat, Ben.'

'Thank you all the same, Mr. Shaughnessy, but I won't be staying more than a minute.' Ben always addressed Mike as Mister Shaughnessy and so drew from Mike in return a definite respect and liking.

'Well, even if you're only going to stay a minute, now that you're here you can take a seat. And perhaps a glass of cider or home-made wine? Lizzie's a dab hand at making home-made wine. I'm sorry I've nothing in the way of a drop of hard to offer you.' Mike smiled ruefully at the old man, attempting to put him at his ease, and Ben, in return, moved his parchment skin in what was for him a smile as he answered, 'Thank you all the same. It's very kind of you but I'll have to be getting back. I just wanted to have a word with you.' He looked from one to the other of them, then added, 'A word with you both.'

When he paused, Mike put in quietly, 'Go ahead then. Go ahead, Ben.'

'It's about Master Tony. He's aiming to leave. He could do it any minute, just go off. He's been getting his things together in a quiet way all this week, and if he goes' – Lizzie watched the muscles of the old man's face twitch as he finished – 'it'll break the master.'

'But why?' Lizzie sat down, and she repeated, 'But why? Why should he want to leave? What's happened, Ben?'

Ben now seemed reluctant to go on. He lowered his head and moved it from side to side before saying, 'The master and he had a few words the other morning. It was from then.'

'What was it over, Ben?' Mike's voice was quiet.

Ben raised his eyes now and looked at Mike, and his lips trembled and his words came stumbling as he said, 'It's a . . . it's a very delicate subject, Mr. Shaughnessy.'

'Let's hear it, Ben.'

'Well, it's this way.' Ben was turning his gaze towards Lizzie at the moment her eyes were being attracted by a dark form entering the court-yard. She was on her feet in a second and, stepping away from the view of the window, whispered hoarsely, 'It's him . . . Mr. Lord.'

At the mention of his master's name Ben started as if he had been shot, and Mike said quickly, 'You can slip out the front way – he'll never know you've been here. Come on.'

As Ben moved across the kitchen there came a sharp rap on the back door. The sound seemed to halt him and, looking at Mike, he said flatly, 'I'm too old to scurry and I don't like running away, not even from him.' He again gave Mike what he considered a smile, and Mike, nodding in approval, said, 'I'll let him in.'

When Mr. Lord entered the kitchen Ben was supporting himself with his hand on the edge of the table, and on the sight of his servant his head went up and he exclaimed in a high, disapproving tone, 'Well! You've strayed, haven't you? What are you doing here?'

Ben's tone was as curt as his master's as he replied, 'I'm visiting . . . I'm visiting my friends. Find fault with that if you can.'

'Since when did you start going out visiting?'

'Since I decided it was high time I took a bit of regular leave. I've hardly been across the door for years and I'm tired of my own company.'

'You're lying. Go on, get up to the house and I'll talk to you later.'

Ben moved slowly across the kitchen, and when he was level with Mr. Lord he straightened his bent shoulders and looked him full in the face, but what remark he was about to make was checked by his master barking at him, 'And you mind your own business. You're an interfering old busybody, as fussy as an old fish-wife. You cause more trouble than enough. Go on, get yourself up to the house.'

Ben's face tightened and his wrinkled chin became a knobbly mat as he declared stoutly, 'You'll go too far one of these days and you'll get a surprise. I'll not only go up, I'll go out . . . I'll clear out.'

'Huh! I wish to heaven you would carry out your threat. Go on, you're only wasting time.' This last was accompanied by a deprecating wave of the hand.

Lizzie listened to this angry exchange between the two old men with her hand on her throat. She felt consumed with sorrow for Ben . . . poor, faithful Ben. On the other hand the exchange almost made Mike laugh. These two had been together so long that they would be like limbless men if the one lost the other. He moved now towards Ben, saying quietly, 'I'll let you out, Ben. Look us up any night, you're always welcome.'

The huh! that escaped from Mr. Lord on hearing this invitation sent them on their way to the back door, where Mike took leave of Ben by patting him on the back and whispering, 'I'll slip in in the morning, Ben, and have a word with you.'

The old man nodded and seemed thankful for the suggestion, and for a moment Mike watched him shambling across the yard before returning to the kitchen.

Mr. Lord was seated on a stiff-backed chair, which seemed to suit his present attitude, for no sooner had Mike entered the room than he demanded, 'Well, what was he after?'

'After? What would he be after? As he said, he had just dropped in to see us.'

'Don't stall, Shaughnessy. He had come down here to talk about Tony, hadn't he? Well, hadn't he?' He now turned his gaze on Lizzie and went on, 'He had come to tell you that the boy was making plans to go off without letting me know, and he must be stopped. Well now, I'll tell you something.' His eyes were on Mike again. 'Let him go, do nothing to stop him. I don't care if I never set eyes on him again.'

His voice had risen and was so full of anger that Lizzie, remembering what his fury had done to him three years ago and the disastrous heart attack that followed, cried, 'Stop now. You don't mean that, Mr. Lord. . . . Let me make you a drink.'

'I do mean it, Mrs. Shaughnessy. That boy is a fool. I should have recognized it in the beginning. He's his grandmother over again – empty-headed, stupid, wilful. . . .'

'Now, sir' – this was Mike speaking quietly – 'you know that isn't true. If it's true of him, then it's true of you, for you're as alike as two peas.'

'Don't start that again, Shaughnessy. He's got no more of me in him than you have. And I'm telling you' – his voice was even higher now – 'he'll not get a farthing, not one brass farthing of mine. I'll leave it to a dog's home . . . cat's home . . . rest home for old horses, anything but people . . . never a penny to him. I swear it. I do . . . I do.'

'Mr. Lord. . . .' Lizzie was standing close by the old man's side as she said, 'I'm going to get you a drink. Will you have a cup of strong coffee?'

Looking up at her, Mr. Lord swallowed twice, then took in a shivering breath before saying in an absolutely changed tone, 'Thank you, Mrs. Shaughnessy, yes, I'd like a cup of coffee.' He glanced towards Mike now and in the form of a polite request he asked him, 'Would you mind going to the car? There's a flask in the right-hand pocket. I always carry a little . . . a little brandy with me.'

After one quick glance at his master, Mike hurried out, and Mr. Lord, with his hand pressed tightly under his ribs, looked at Lizzie again and asked quietly, 'Did your husband tell you of the conversation we had the other morning regarding . . . regarding Mary Ann's future?'

Lizzie's eyes widened just a fraction and she shook her head.

'Well, that's what all the trouble is about.'

'Trouble?' As Lizzie repeated the word a wave of fear sped through her. Somehow she had known all the time that this business was wrapped up with Mary Ann. But she couldn't understand Mike knowing about it and not mentioning it to her, or, as was usual when the old man showed more than a little interest in Mary Ann's future, going off the deep end about it.

Mr. Lord took in another deep breath before he said, and softer still now, 'I thought he might have told you.'

At that moment Mike came hurrying into the kitchen, a flask in his hand, and going straight to the dresser and taking a glass from the rack he poured out a generous measure of the brandy and handed it to his master, who took it without a word and sipped at it slowly for a few moments. 'You didn't tell your wife,' he said, 'what we discussed the other morning, Shaughnessy?'

Mike flashed a quick look at Lizzie's back. 'No, sir,' he replied, 'I didn't think there was any need.'

'Well, she had better know as it concerns her. It concerns us all. As I've just told her, it's the cause of all the trouble.' He took another sip of the brandy and, looking down into the glass where he had rested it on the corner of the table, he said, 'Perhaps I was a bit too hasty after all, but I thought the boy still had an interest in that Johnson girl. I told him I was going down that morning to tell them they must vacate the cottage as soon as possible to make way for another man coming in, and he told me I couldn't do it, it was cold-blooded.'

'And so it would have been.' Mike's voice was stiff.

144

Mr. Lord continued to look down into the remains of the brandy in the glass as he went on, 'Johnson was engaged weekly, I owe him nothing but a week's wages. I was going to be generous and give him a month's pay in lieu of notice, but even that didn't suit my socialistic-minded grandson, and one word led to another. And then, I'm afraid, I lost my temper and I told him that if he saw that girl again I would put the family out on the road. I also told him what I told you that particular morning.'

'Oh Lord!' Mike was not addressing Mr. Lord, he was groaning aloud, and, looking at his employer square, he said bluntly, 'Well, sir, I thought you would have had more sense.'

Lizzie clutched the front of her dress and waited for Mr. Lord's response, and when it came it surprised her, for there was no lightning change of tone. 'Yes, Shaughnessy, I should have thought so myself. But there, it was done, and if I had told him he mustn't marry for five years because I had a rich widow lined up for him he could not have reacted in a worse manner.'

'And I don't blame him.'

'Would you mind telling me what all this is about?'

Lizzie looked from one to the other, and Mr. Lord, after returning her inquiring glance, had the grace to bow his head and leave the telling to Mike.

'It's just like this, Liz.' Mike paused, and his face was tight and his brows meeting as he went, 'Mr. Lord proposes that Tony doesn't marry for the next five years, in fact until Mary Ann is seventeen. I leave the rest to your imagination.'

Lizzie's hand moved up from the front of her dress to her mouth. Mary Ann had inherited her squeamish stomach from her mother, and now Lizzie felt her whole inside heave. For the moment she saw the suggestion as something nasty . . . dirty . . . even obscene. Mary Ann was still a child. But no, Mary Ann had been thirteen on Wednesday, she was a young girl. Yet she was still only a child – of course she was a child – and there he was planning for her to marry a man nearly ten years older than herself. It was true . . . it was shocking . . . like the things you read about, like they did in foreign countries, marrying children in their cradles.

The voice of sensibility again intruded into Lizzie's mind, saying, Mary Ann is thirteen, and girls are mothers at sixteen and before.

'You don't take kindly to the idea, Mrs. Shaughnessy?'

'No, sir, I don't. I think . . . I think . . .' Lizzie's lips trembled and she couldn't tell the old man what she thought. And when Mike put her thoughts into words for her she was more amazed still by the calmness of his manner.

'She's a bit shocked, sir,' he said.

'I'll have that cup of coffee now, Mrs. Shaughnessy, if I may.'

Silently Lizzie poured out the coffee and placed it at his elbow, and as she watched him drink she wondered, among other things, how he could swallow it so hot. When the cup was empty and not one of them had spoken for some moments, Mr. Lord rose slowly to his feet and, looking from Mike to Lizzie, he said quietly, 'You're nice people. Others would have looked upon the proposition as a good thing, for if I don't disinherit my grandson part of his assets should be around two hundred thousand pounds when I die. Thank you for the coffee, Mrs. Shaughnessy.'

'You're welcome, sir.' Lizzie's voice was very small.

Mr. Lord took three steps towards the door before turning to them both again, saying, 'I'd better tell you my other bit of news while I'm at it. I had a talk with Bristow and he tells me Johnson is determined to make quite a bit out of this affair. By the way, his ankle is fractured, which makes the case against you blacker. He can be off work from anything up to a month or more, you can never tell with a fracture. If he goes to the County Court and wins you might get off with a couple of hundred – anyway, he can't get more than four hundred there – but if it goes to the Sessions there's no knowing what you'll be run in for. . . . Now don't say anything, Shaughnessy—' Mr. Lord lifted his hand in a gesture now as if he was tired, and Mike refrained from making any comment. 'Bristow says the best thing to do will be to settle out of court, and I agree with him. I took it upon myself, Shaughnessy, to ask him to probe the matter and find out how much Johnson will settle for. And whatever it is I'll see to it; the quicker this thing is done the better. Once a case like this starts to drag on there's no knowing where it'll end. Now please' – he again made a gesture – 'let me do this. I owe it to you, anyway. I would have paid much more than they are likely to ask to get that girl away from the place. Really it's Mary Ann who should be paid a lump sum and a studded collar given to Neptune.' He gave a weary smile. Then his head drooped forward and, in a voice that had a muttering quality, he said, 'There's one thing I would ask of you, and you'll think I'm in my dotage after what I said previously this evening, but if you could talk to the boy and make him see sense I'd be obliged, Shaughnessy.'

He remained for a moment longer, with his eyes downcast. Then, raising them to Lizzie, he said, 'Good night, Mrs. Shaughnessy.'

'Good night, sir.'

'It's all right, Shaughnessy, I can see myself out.'

'If it's all the same to you, sir, I'll walk with you as far as the house. I've got to do the round in any case.'

Again Mr. Lord turned to Lizzie, and again he said, 'Good night.'

'Good night, sir.'

Slowly Lizzie sat down by the side of the table. The mixture in the boat-shaped tins had gone flat and lost its rising quality. She stared at it, her fingers across her mouth. Was there ever such a strange man? Planning to marry Mary Ann to Tony. No wonder Tony had kept away from them. . . . And Mike taking it all so calmly, she couldn't understand that. And then the old man going to pay that sum of money, which, by the sound of it, wouldn't be small. She couldn't make him out, he did the most contrary things. . . . But planning to marry Mary Ann off at her age . . . well, really!

As she sat pondering over the matter the door leading from the hall opened and Michael came in, a stack of books in his arms.

'Did I hear Mr. Lord come in?' he asked.

Lizzie looked up at him, and then she smiled tenderly at

her son as she said, 'Yes, he's been in, talking to your father.'

Michael did not ask what Mr. Lord had wanted, nor had Michael been listening. Michael was not Mary Ann.

He placed the books on the couch and, stretching his arms above his head, he exclaimed, 'Oh, I'm tired.'

'I'll get you a drink. What would you like, cocoa or Horlicks?'

Michael did not answer Lizzie's question but bent over the couch again and sorted his books into a neat pile before saying quietly, 'I saw Sarah Flannagan tonight, Ma.'

'Did you? Where was she?'

'On a pony along the road. . . . Ma—'

'Yes?' Lizzie stood at the stove.

'Can I bring her over to tea tomorrow?'

'Michael!' Lizzie had swung round as if she had been scalded.

'All right. All right. I only asked.'

There was his father speaking and Lizzie, looking at his bent, flushed face, said, 'You know, Michael, I wouldn't mind in the least, but just think how she'll take on. And you know it's her party.'

'Has she always to have her own way?'

'Oh, now, that's unfair!'

'It isn't, Ma, and you know it. If she sets out to get her own way she gets it in the end, or there's hell to pay.'

'Michael! Now don't you use words like that. Really!'

'I'm sorry, Ma, but you see—' He ran his hand through his hair. 'Well, I want Sarah to come here. I want her to see you. I want her to see us all in this house.' He spread his arms wide and kept them there during the moment of silence that followed. Then letting them flap to his sides he exclaimed, 'And that's not all ... I ... I like her, Ma.'

Lizzie looked hard at her son. Michael had never bothered with girls. He was a sensible, level-headed boy, but she knew that if he said he liked Sarah Flannagan, then he liked her and he wouldn't be put off her. Yet why had it to be Sarah Flannagan? Oh dear, oh dear, the emotional upsets in the family during these last two weeks were beyond belief.

Hadn't she enough to think about with this business of Mary Ann and Tony without Michael starting on about Sarah Flannagan? What was happening to everybody?

Her mind swung back to Wednesday and the memory of Mary Ann coming back to Mrs. McBride's crying her eyes out. Well, at any rate that business of the clothes had been a blessing in disguise . . . she wouldn't have to worry about Corny Boyle turning up with people like Mrs. Willoughby rolling to the door in her car to deposit her daughter, and Mrs. Schofield bringing her Janice, not to mention the other four. . . . She said now to Michael, out of the blue, 'Is she presentable?'

'Presentable, Ma? She's smashing. She's the best-looking girl going.'

'Sarah Flannagan?'

'Yes, Ma, Sarah Flannagan. It's years since you saw her. She's different, with lovely black hair, and she's nearly as tall as me.'

'Well, all that isn't going to placate Mary Ann any. Whether you realize it or not, your sister's touchy about her height, and if Miss Flannagan' – now Lizzie's tone was slightly sarcastic – 'and if Miss Flannagan's as tall as you, then Mary Ann is going to be at a still greater disadvantage, isn't she?'

'Look, Ma. Don't take it like that, please.' His voice sounded hurt.

'Oh, I'm sorry, son, I'm tired. But I still don't think it'll be wise to bring Sarah tomorrow.'

'If you think Mary Ann will be put to a disadvantage by Sarah, think again, Ma. Have you ever known her be at a disadvantage with anybody? If she is it only makes her show off the more.'

'All right, all right, don't keep on. Look, it's late, get yourself off to bed, we'll talk about it in the morning. Good night.'

'Good night, Ma.' He kissed her gently and went out. Lizzie sat down again. She was tired. Oh, she was tired; she would just like to go upstairs this minute and go to bed. That batch of mixture was no good now. Well, there'd be piles of stuff for everybody; she had baked enough to serve at a wedding. She wished Mike would hurry up and come in.

As if in answer to her wish she heard him coming in the back-door, but she closed her eyes wearily when she realized that he wasn't alone.

'Hallo, Lizzie.' Tony was standing just inside the kitchen door.

'Hallo, Tony. Come and sit down.' Lizzie blinked her tiredness away. 'Will you have a cup of something? The coffee's still hot . . . a cup of coffee?'

'As you like.' Tony's voice was subdued.

Mike was striding about the room now and she could not make out whether his annoyance was real or simulated when he said, 'Sit yourself down there, you're not moving out of here until we get things straight. Pour me one out, Liz, when you're on. Make it black, I've got a lot of talking to do.'

Lizzie poured out not only two cups of coffee but three. And having handed the two men theirs, she sat by the table listening, not to Tony, for he still hadn't spoken, but to Mike, and she soon found that without the aid of the coffee she was wide awake, for Mike was talking as she had never heard him talk before, at least when he was discussing his daughter.

'As I told the old man the other morning, Tony, if Mary Ann wants you she'll have you, and if she doesn't want you the devil in hell won't make her take you, not if you were hung round with the two hundred thousand the old man says you're likely to get.'

'He told you that?'

'Yes, and don't go off the deep end again.'

'Oh, but, Mike, it's nothing but that all the time, holding out bait. Look, I would stay and gladly and I don't need any bait. I hadn't thought about leaving him, not until the other morning.'

'Well, you can forget that,' Mike put in quickly. 'And I'm telling you something that the old man is blind to: he's blind to the fact that all the grooming in the world, all the grammar learning, all the mixing with the right people' – Mike gave this particular word great stress – 'cannot change the blood in your veins. If Mary Ann lives to be eighty and she marries into the top drawer, let me tell you this, Tony: she will remain a child of the Tyne. I don't know much about psychology and that sort of clatter, but I do know the first ten years of your life counts. I know that from experience. I know that from what I've seen in others. Have you ever thought of some of the pitmen and dockers from around these quarters who have risen and become Members of Parliament. Some of them come back and live on their old doorsteps. The others that don't and live in their big houses, what do they talk about among their friends? They talk about the past, their boyhood in the pits or in the shipyard. I tell you, Tony, a man or a woman are their first ten years. Look at me. I've got a good job now, a wife second to none, a good home and two children that I'm proud of. My dreams should be pleasant. Yet I wake up in the night and I'm back in the bare, stone-walled dormitory in the workhouse. And mind, that memory goes back to well before I was five because I was in the Cottage Homes from I was five.'

'Oh, Mike.' Tony moved his head and, his voice filled with concern, he murmured, 'I didn't mean to make you talk . . .'

'Look here, don't get me wrong,' Mike interrupted him. 'I'm not plugging any sob line, I'm just trying to explain to you that Mary Ann is not going to be the product of the old boy. I realized this three years ago when she ran away from the convent, and it's helped my peace of mind since. Why, lad, I can laugh at his schemings, and you've got to an' all. The thing is you've got to play up to him. He's an old autocrat of the first water; if you let him get you rattled you're done. I know that from experience an' all. But if you play him, things'll run along slowly. So there, I've told you. And if you leave here don't let it be on account of the child. If you stay, let the old man have his dream. Only remember, his awakening lies with Mary Ann.'

'I wish I could see things your way, Mike.' Tony sighed. 'But the snag is I'm with him most of the time and he'll keep on about it, alluding to it. I don't think I could stand it. I might tell you I've never had such a shock in my life as when he blurted it out the other morning.' He turned now and looked at Lizzie, then added by way of explanation, 'It all started because he had seen me bringing the parcel down on Sunday, he wanted to know what was in it. By the way, did the things fit him?'

It was Lizzie's turn to drop her head. 'He wouldn't accept them, Tony.'

'No?'

'It was nothing personal . . .'

'That's just what it was, Liz,' Mike put in abruptly. 'Don't try to paint the situation. It was like this, Tony. The lad saw you and the old man as the boys with the money, and as I understand it the old man didn't hide how he felt about him. It got under the lad's skin, and I can understand that very well an' all. So he wouldn't accept your charity. Apparently he's a lad who thinks for himself, and he thinks along the lines that whatever he's going to wear it's not coming off somebody else's back. I don't expect you to understand that, Tony.'

'Oh, but I do, Mike, I do. And I like the boy all the more for it. Still, it's a pity in a way, as it'll be one less at her party.' It was the first time he had alluded directly to Mary Ann, and he smiled now as he went on, 'And I somehow think he would have been the guest of honour.'

Mike laughed at this, but Lizzie's face remained straight, and Tony, looking at her, said, 'You've no idea how I've missed coming in.' Then getting abruptly to his feet added, 'Well, I must be off; he'll be waiting up for me. That's another thing that gets under my skin – he never goes to bed until I come in.'

Lizzie now walked over to Tony and, standing in front of him, looked at him keenly as she said, 'I don't think you realize, Tony, just how much you mean to him. Since you came into his life it's as if he had been reborn again. In fact he said as much to me in this very kitchen. I'm going to say this, Tony, and it mightn't please you, but I don't think you really understand him. You don't try. You're still carrying the handicap of being brought up by someone who didn't like him.' Lizzie's voice dropped low at this stage as she added, 'And in our own family we know the damage a grandmother can do. It would be a good thing if you would try to see his side of you.'

'But I do, Lizzie, I do. Mike knows—' he turned his eyes towards Mike, '—he knows the things I put up with from him.'

Lizzie shook her head impatiently. 'Those are external things, his shouting, his bossing, all the things he uses as a cover-up for his real feelings. But you haven't given him anything of yourself, Tony. Don't ask me how I know this, but I do, and if you search your conscience you'll admit I'm right. You are tolerant with him but you've never shown him any love, never. Now have you?'

Tony's eyes moved downwards and then across the darkening room to the window, and there was a long pause before he answered, 'It's difficult; he pushes you off.'

'That's just his manner, his armour, a protection he has built about himself against people over the last forty years. He was hurt so badly that even at this late stage he's terrified of it being repeated. Why do you think he's planning for you and Mary Ann? It's just to keep you near him in case you should marry somebody who will whisk you away. He knows something of Mary Ann and her love and loyalty, and he knows that he holds a share in that loyalty, and if for no other reason than that Mary Ann would keep you with him to the end. . . . Try to understand.'

Slowly Tony brought his eyes back to Lizzie, and after a moment of staring at her he turned away, saying quietly, 'Good night, Lizzie.' Then looking towards Mike, he said, 'Good night, Mike . . . and thanks.'

As the door closed on him they looked at each other and almost at the same time they both sighed. Then Lizzie, watching Mike make for his chair, said with startling abruptness, 'Don't sit yourself down, for I'm not going to talk about her, or Tony, or the old man, or anything else tonight. I'm dropping on my feet. And I've all this place to clean up and tomorrow facing me, and I can tell you I'm not looking forward to it.'

Answering not a word, Mike, with one hand, lifted the laden tray from the table and, balancing it expertly, carried it into the scullery. Could you get over women, or understand their reactions. Just a matter of minutes ago Liz had heard that the old man was planning to marry her daughter off to his heir, and she didn't want to talk about it . . . she wanted to clear away. Could you beat it?

CHAPTER TWELVE

THE PARTY

THE sun was shining, the house was shining, and the table now stretching across the farm kitchen was shining with its white cloth and best china laden with food. The sitting-room door was wide open, its windows were wide open, and there were flowers in the fireplace. Mary Ann had personally seen to this touch. Michael was wearing his best suit, and Lizzie was wearing a new dress which made Mike think to himself, as he was wont to do at times, 'She's beautiful, is Liz.'

Lizzie was moving up and down the table, adjusting a plate here, a napkin there. After she had made the round of the table three times and was now at the side table going through the same process with the dishes of trifle and fruit, Mike exclaimed, on a laugh, 'Let up, Liz, or you'll snap! What you tensed up about, anyway – the young 'uns, or those who'll be bringing 'em?'

When Lizzie did not answer, he went on, 'Just you remember, my girl, you can hold your own with the best. It's me who should be worrying about meeting the gentry, not you. But perhaps you're worrying because of me, eh?'

'Oh, don't be silly, Mike.' Lizzie turned about and faced him and then laughed as she admitted, 'I don't know what's the matter with me, I'm all on edge. And she's not making me any better; it's as if she didn't want the party. She's not herself, hasn't been all day. Other time she'd be bouncing about the place and you couldn't knock her down if you tried.'

'Where is she?'

It was Michael who answered his father, saying, 'She's at the gate waiting.'

As Mike went out of the kitchen and through the hall towards the front door Michael turned to Lizzie and asked, 'Did you say anything to her about what I said last night?'

'No I didn't, Michael.'

'Well, I'm bringing her, Ma.'

'Now, Michael. . . .'

'Well, I can't get out of it now, I've asked her.'

'Oh!' It was a loud exclamation of impatience. 'You're another one lashing out with invitations without thinking. You made game and criticized her for inviting Corny, and now you go and do something similar yourself.'

'Oh, Ma, hold on, you can't compare Sarah with Corny Boyle. Good Lord!'

'That's just a matter of opinion. Now be quiet, listen! Is that a car?'

As Lizzie made her way quickly to the hall Michael cried after her, 'Well mind, Ma, I'm going to risk it and bring her. If our Mary Ann shows off and causes a scene that'll be her look-out.'

Michael's voice trailed away from Lizzie's hearing as she reached the front door. When she caught sight of the car drawing to a stop at the gate her heart began to pound nervously.

'Oh, Mary Ann.'

'Oh, hallo, Beatrice. I am pleased to see you.' Mary Ann was doing the honours. 'How do you do, Mrs. Willoughby? Mrs. Willoughby, this is my mother.'

'How do you do?' said Lizzie, inclining her head forward.

'I'm very pleased to meet you,' said Mrs. Willoughby.

That was funny. . . . This thought nipped into the proceedings and presented itself to Mary Ann. It was funny that it should be her ma who should say 'How do you do?' and Mrs. Willoughby who should say 'I'm pleased to meet you'; the correct greeting should have been 'How do you do?' – she had learned that much long ago in Sister Catherine's social sessions.

'This is my husband.'

Mrs. Willoughby was shaking hands with Mike, and if her expression was anything to go by she was quite impressed with the big red-headed man.

'Oh, isn't it lovely here? Oh, what a pretty house you have, Mary Ann.' Beatrice was gushing aloud, and she turned to her mother and said, 'Isn't it lovely, Mummy?'

'Yes, delightful.'

'Won't you stay and have a cup of tea?' Lizzie was smiling. The ice was broken and she was feeling just a little more at ease.

'Thank you, but no, I have an appointment in town this afternoon. But some other time I would love to, if I may.'

Mrs. Willoughby sounded as if she meant what she said, and as Lizzie looked at the expensively dressed woman her nervousness left her completely. What was she, after all, but just another woman, just another ma. She became calm inside and rather proud, because now Mike was opening the door of the car for Mrs. Willoughby and there was a natural air about him that many a man in a better position would have envied.

'I'm afraid you'll have to back down here and turn in at the farm gate, the road's rather narrow and a bit rough.'

Mike was bending down to Mrs. Willoughby, and she smiled widely at him as she replied, 'Oh, that's all right, I'll manage, Mr. Shaughnessy.' She put the gears into reverse and then added, 'Good-bye for the present, I'll see you later.'

But Mrs. Willoughby hadn't backed the car as far as the farm gate when another car, coming at a tearing rate, made its appearance round the bend, and it was followed by yet another one.

In a low aside to Lizzie Mike now exclaimed in thick dialect, 'Aalltegither like the folk o' Shields.'

'Mike!' It was a warning from Lizzie, and Mike laughed and went forward to the traffic jam that was building up outside the farm gate.

'Why couldn't you stay up on the broad part of the road, Lettice?' Mrs. Willoughby was leaning out of her car and calling to Janice's mother now, and this gaily attired individual, thrusting her head out of the window, cried, 'Swing her round, darling, you'll take the gate-post up in a minute. Give me a couple of inches and I'll get by . . .'

'Oh, you are a fool, Lettice!' Mrs. Willoughby sounded more than a little annoyed, until Mike, coming to her side, guided her clear of the heavy gate-post with the iron latch protruding from it, saying, 'Over a bit. A little more left. That's it, that's it, you're through now.' He bent down towards her and advised, 'I'd stay put for a second or so until the others get past.'

The third car was being driven by an extremely fat lady with a replica of herself sitting at her side, and Mrs. Willoughby, looking up at Mike, asked, 'Who is that?'

'I haven't the foggiest notion.' Mike's eyes were twinkling. 'But the child's likely another . . . dear friend of Mary Ann's.'

Returning Mike's twinkle, Mrs. Willoughby laughed softly now. Connie hadn't exaggerated when she said that the Shaughnessy man had points, he certainly had. She wished she'd been able to accept the invitation to tea. She could also see where the attraction lay for Bob – the child's mother was a most arresting woman, and without any artificial aid at that.

'There you are, all clear now.' Mike guided Mrs. Willoughby's car into the road again and waved her good-bye before walking back towards the house gate.

'This is my husband, Mrs. Schofield.'

'Oh . . . hallo, Mr. Shaughnessy, I've heard such a lot about you. Janice talks about Mary Ann from morning till night, and Mary Ann talks about you. You see, it's like jungle telegraph . . . you're just like I pictured you. And you, too, Mrs. Shaughnessy. I knew before I clapped eyes on you that you had marvellous blonde hair and were beautiful.'

'Oh, Mrs. Schofield.' Lizzie was definitely embarrassed, but she had to laugh – they all laughed. She could see that Mrs. Schofeld was a sort of character – a cross between a Mrs. Feather and a Blondie. 'Will you stay and have a cup of tea, Mrs. Schofield?'

'Yes, of course I'll stay to tea, and thank you, Mrs. Shaughnessy.'

'Oh, Mammy, you don't have to stay—' This was Janice addressing her mother in horrified tones. 'It's a girls' party.'

'Away with you! I'm still a girl . . . aren't I, Mr. Shaughnessy?' She spoke as if she had known Mike all her life, and Mike replied gallantly, 'And you will be all your life, Mrs. Schofield.'

The laughter filled the front garden. It surrounded Mary Ann and should have made her heart glad: everything was going like a house afire, everyone was so nice.

'What did you say, Beatrice?' She turned to Beatrice who had whispered something to her.

'Where's Michael?' Beatrice was looking quite coy, and Mary Ann, in a manner more off-hand than she should have used to a guest, and to her best friend into the bargain, said, 'Oh, he's about somewhere.'

'I've brought you this, Mary Ann. I hope you'll like it.' The fat girl was now holding out a long, gaily-covered box to Mary Ann, and Mary Ann, taking it, gushed, 'Oh, thank you, Betty. Oh, that is sweet of you. Oh, I'll love it.' Later she wondered why Betty had to give her a bath puff with a long handle when you could sprinkle talcum all over you from any fancy container.

'Here's another car. Oh, it's Alec Moore.' Janice, definitely excited, forgot about her mother's intrusion and joined Mary Ann at the gate.

The car not only held Alec Moore but Roy Connor and a boy little bigger than Mary Ann, called Dennis Braton. They were all smartly dressed, bright-eyed, and they all carried parcels which in turn they dutifully handed to Mary Ann.

'Oh, thank you, thank you. Oh, that is kind of you. Look, Mother – look what the boys have given me.' Not only Mike and Lizzie looked, but everyone crowded around to admire the presents. No one had moved from the vicinity of the gate, but the party had certainly begun.

It was in full swing when Tony arrived. He came round the front of the house where the deck-chairs were scattered on the lawn. He stopped near Mike and was introduced by him to Mrs. Schofield, who immediately invited him to take a seat near her. After a courtly bow, which would have pleased his grandfather, and with words to the effect that he would defer the pleasure until he had seen Mary Ann, he went in search of her.

'Isn't he lovely? Who is he? Oh, he's charming.'

As Mike looked down on Mrs. Schofield and gave her the necessary information he wondered to himself how such women as this ever came to be married, and, further still, how they managed to be mothers. And yet, he concluded with a quiet laugh, rabbits managed that function all right.

'Do you know, I used to dream about being a farmer's wife, Mr. Shaughnessy?'

'Really?'

'Yes, really and truly. Honest. Honest, I'm not joking. But perhaps I'm not quite the type. What do you think?'

Mike, chuckling inwardly, was taking the bait when Mary Ann, rushing from the house, cried excitedly, 'Father! Father!' For the moment he did not realize that the title was meant for him, and when he did it was as much as he could do to stop himself from bellowing aloud, 'Father, indeed!' It was the first time she had ever called him that.

'Look . . . look what Tony has given me.' She lifted up from the front of her dress a gold cross on a thin gold chain. 'Isn't it lovely?'

'Yes . . . By, it's beautiful! Did you thank him?'

'Oh yes. Yes, of course.' She looked from Mike to Mrs. Schofield for a moment, then back to Mike again. She wanted to say, 'Tony's all right now,' but this wasn't the place, and Mrs. Schofield was such a funny woman that she would likely want to know if he had been bad or something. She hadn't imagined Janice having such a funny mother; she didn't think she would like a mother like Mrs. Schofield.

'Well, well, we're all excitement.'

Mike, Mary Ann and Mrs. Schofield turned towards the deep voice of Mr. Lord, and Mike, pulling a straight garden chair forward, said, 'Good afternoon, sir. Will you have a seat? This is Mrs. Schofield. Mr. Lord, Mrs. Schofield.'

'How do you do?'

Mrs. Schofield was reminded of the young man through the way this old one inclined his thin body towards her.

'I'm very well, very well. Do sit down, I've heard such a lot about you. My father-in-law used to be connected with Redheads.'

'Did he? No, I won't take a seat yet awhile. . . . Hallo, Mary Ann.'

'Hallo, Mr. Lord.'

'A happy birthday to you, Mary Ann.'

'Thank you, Mr. Lord.' She smiled at him a welcoming smile, for she was genuinely pleased to see him. Tony and he must be all right or he wouldn't have come. She watched him look towards the road. Then when he looked back at her he asked, 'Have you had a lot of nice birthday presents?'

'Oh yes, some lovely ones. Look, Tony gave me this cross.' She held the cross up to him.

'Yes, very nice, very nice.' He nodded at her and she smiled at him again. He hadn't given her a present, but that didn't matter, he spent lots of money in other ways. She had, she knew, much to be grateful to him for, and when he was nice, as now, she was grateful. She didn't want a present from him.

He looked to where the boys and girls were searching among the bushes, and Mary Ann explained, 'We're having a treasure hunt.'

He nodded, then said, 'You have a lot of nice friends, Mary Ann.'

She did not smile at him now, for she was seeing the picture of Corny standing on the pavement saying, 'I'll get on. By God, I'll get on!' and she shuddered a little as in thought she took the Lord's name in vain.

Mr. Lord now looked at his watch, and then from Mary Ann to Mike before he said, 'I'm expecting someone.'

'Yes, sir?' Mike looked inquiringly at the old man.

'They should be here any minute.'

Mary Ann looked slightly startled, for she too was expecting someone, in fact two someones. It was this fact that contributed to her nervousness all day.

She was uneasy about a number of things; she wasn't happy although she was trying her hardest to pretend to be. On the surface she had every reason to be happy, for her party was going with a swing and promised to be an enormous success and the subject of conversation for many days to come. And she had proof of this as she looked at her young guests dashing uninhibited about the garden and the house. Even their Michael had joined in, Beatrice had seen to that. A thought intruded at this point to ask what was up with their Michael? He had been looking at her funnily all day. But she couldn't waste time at this stage on Michael and what was up with him, for Mr. Lord was saying and in an odd way, 'Any minute. Any minute now.'

Her attention was lifted from him to the road once again by the arrival of yet another car and her da exclaiming, 'Not another! I thought we'd had the lot.'

When the car stopped at the gate and Bob Quinton alighted Mike assumed the right reactions towards this visitor. He remained quiet and kept his face straight, and this was rather difficult to do when he saw his daughter's agitation. At the same time he kept his glance on Lizzie as she greeted Bob, wondering in spite of all he knew to the contrary if she would be affected at the sight of him, and if this perhaps had been the actual cause of her nervousness all day. But he could see nothing in her attitude but feigned surprise.

'Why, hallo, Bob. Well, what's brought you up here today?'

'Oh, hallo there, Lizzie. Hallo, Mike. Hallo, Mary Ann.' Bob made the greetings before he gave Lizzie an answer and then he added with a side-long glance at Mary Ann, 'I just happened to be passing along the top of the road and I thought: I haven't seen the Shaughnessys for years.' He spread his eyes now around the garden and said, 'I'm sorry, I've butted in at the wrong time. I didn't know you were having a party.'

'It's Mary Ann's birthday, Bob, but you're very welcome, and you must stay and have a cup of tea.'

'I'd like that, Lizzie, thanks.' He was turning to Mike

when a voice from the garden exclaimed in high excited tones, 'Why, Bob, what a delight!'

Mike heard the groan that Bob gave as he walked towards Mrs. Schofield's chair, saying, 'Hallo there, Lettice. Well, well, fancy seeing you out in the country.'

As Mary Ann watched Mrs. Schofield hanging on to Mr. Quinton's arm and listened to her high, laughing, jocular remarks, it crossed her mind that if Mrs. Quinton did come she wouldn't get much chance to make it up with Mr. Quinton if Mrs. Schofield was still about, and her sympathy deepened for Janice. No wonder Janice said her mother was a drip. The term had rather horrified Mary Ann, but she could see Janice's point.

'Hallo there, Quinton; you lost?' Mr. Lord's voice was terse.

'No, no, sir; just paying a visit to old friends. How are you?'

'I'm well, thank you.'

Mary Ann was puzzled by Mr. Lord's attitude, for all the time he talked to Mr. Quinton he kept glancing up the road. And, moreover, he wouldn't let her away but told her to wait a moment, for he wanted her. Then even as she was wondering what on earth he could be wanting her for – he couldn't possibly be about to go for her in front of everybody – he gave a loud 'Aah!' and crossed the lawn to the gate, saying as he did so, 'Mary Ann . . . Mary Ann, come here.'

When Mary Ann stood by his side in the middle of the road and looked along it, she was looking into the sun and all she could see for the moment was the outline of a horse. And when the horse came into the first shadow of the farm buildings, sharp indignation ran through her. It was not only a horse she was seeing but, of all people . . . Sarah Flannagan! The cheek. What did she want here?

Sarah was not riding the horse – pony would be the more correct term – she was leading it. It was small and a piebald, and even at a distance looked a beauty. But Mary Ann was not concerned with the horse. What was Sarah Flannagan doing here? They were not alone now on the road; all the grown-ups were standing around the gate, and some of the younger guests, out of curiosity, had joined them. But Mary Ann had eyes for no one but Sarah Flannagan. Daring to come to her party and bring her horse!

Then her indignation was supplanted by stark surprise, threaded with not a little fear, for as the two unexpected guests advanced nearer Mr. Lord greeted Sarah in a kind voice, saying, 'There you are. You got here, and on time. Good girl.'

Mr. Lord knew Sarah Flannagan, he was talking to her as if he liked her. For a second Mary Ann was consumed by a blinding feeling of jealousy, a feeling that only a year ago would have prompted her arms and legs into battle.

Everyone about her was exclaiming on the beauty of the pony until Mr. Lord silenced them with uplifted hand. Then, taking the bridle from Sarah, he turned about and, looking at Mary Ann, who was at the moment not wearing her best face, said, 'This, Mary Ann, is your birthday present.'

'Eh?' The ejaculation was shot out of her in surprise. 'For me? Mine? . . . Oh no!' She shook her head.

'You don't like him? You don't want him?'

Her gaping mouth closed and her eyes lifted in amazement from the pony to Mr. Lord's face, and she cried, 'Yes, oh yes. But a horse! I never . . . never . . .' She turned her head first one way and saw her mother, and then the other way and saw Mike, exclaiming now, 'Oh, Ma! Oh, Da!' at the same time knowing that the use of such familiar terms was no way to repay Mr. Lord for his kindness. And as she could think of no words which would express her feelings she just flung herself impetuously at him and reached her arms up round his neck.

'There now, there now, that's enough.' Although he blustered, she knew he was pleased. And as she held on to the pony's bridle with one hand she held on to him with the other.

They were surrounded now by the company, and Sarah was in the middle of the circle standing close to Mary Ann. Discovering herself looking straight into the eyes of her old enemy, there seemed nothing for it at this particular moment but to smile, and she heard herself saying as if she was talking to one of her best friends, 'Oh, he's lovely, and thanks for bringing him. I'll have to learn to ride. What's his name?'

'He hasn't got one, we just called him Nip 'cos he's nippy on his legs; but Mr. Lord said you'd give him a name yourself.'

'Yes, yes.' She did not know what to say next to this new Sarah Flannagan, but she knew what she should have said to show her complete magnanimity when she heard her mother say, 'You must stay to tea, Sarah.'

'Thanks, Mrs. Shaughnessy, I'd like to.'

'There you are, you never told me.' It was their Michael speaking to Sarah now, and everybody listening. 'I was going to the bus for you. Why didn't you tell me?'

'I wasn't supposed to.'

Michael was looking at Sarah with unveiled admiration; and as Mary Ann thought, Our Michael's clean gone on her, she found to her surprise that this no longer made her angry.

Whereas Mary Ann was no longer feeling angry, Mike was now having difficulty in suppressing this emotion. For as much as Mr. Lord's gift had delighted Mary Ann it had angered him, and for two reasons. The first being that he always resented the old man giving her lavish presents; the second one was that the old man had forestalled him. For some time now, since Lizzie had first suggested it would be nice if Mary Ann learned to ride at the new school that had opened, an idea had been growing in his mind that it would be nicer still if she had her own pony, and he had thought, 'I'll get her one; as soon as she can ride I'll get her one.' And now the old man had stepped in before him. . . .

'Remember what you told me last night, Mike?'

Mike turned his head sharply to look at Tony. The young man was smiling quizzically at him, and now with his voice very low he said, 'You must practise what you preach, you know.'

On a sudden Mike laughed. He put out his fist and punched Tony, and Tony, looking over Mike's shoulder, said under his breath, 'He's wanting you.'

When Mike turned and looked at Mr. Lord over the heads

of the crowd the old man, making unusual deference to Mike's position, said, 'Will the top field behind the house be all right to put him in, Shaughnessy?'

'Yes. Yes, that will be quite all right.'

'Well, you put her up then.' Mr. Lord looked at Mike as if he were asking a favour. He had never been as soft-toned before, to Mike's knowledge.

Mr. Lord was indeed in a good frame of mind this afternoon. The boy had seen sense, and he had just given Mary Ann the present he had been considering for some time and which would give her the opportunity to enjoy the pastime of a young lady. Moreover, he had, by a word to Shaughnessy, got the animal housed in the field behind his house, which would ensure that he saw the child daily; for although she visited him often there were days when he didn't see her at all. Yes, he was in a very good frame of mind.

With a swing of his arm Mike lifted Mary Ann into the saddle, and when she was seated on what appeared to her the top of the world, so high was she from the ground, she did not look at the pony but straight into Mike's eyes, and she whispered, 'Oh, Da!'

Aw well – Mike smiled reassuredly to himself – as he was always saying, it would take a lot to change her. In spite of all her fancy friends it took just a little real emotion to turn him into her da again. With a pat on her knee and directions to Michael, who was at one side of the pony's head for the sole reason that Sarah was at the other, he sent his daughter on her perilous but triumphant ride down the road and through into the farm-yard, which was the shortest way to the field at the top of the hill, and the whole company followed.

Mike was now walking with Mrs. Schofield, and Lizzie was a few steps behind accompanied by Bob Quinton. Being the last of the procession, they were just turning into the farm-yard when Lizzie stopped, her glance caught by a solitary figure walking along the road. Seeing her hesitate, Bob too turned his gaze along the road, and then his steps jerked to a halt and he stood staring.

Lizzie's mind was in a whirl. The woman coming towards

her was a stranger, she had never seen her in her life before and yet she knew her. She saw immediately that she was extremely smart, one of those women who could afford to dress with the utmost simplicity, in fact the type that was made outstanding by simplicity. Her dress and hat were grey, and her shoes were navy. They were nothing in themselves, there was nothing much about them, and yet it looked as though she had stepped out of a plate-glass window.

'Hallo, Connie.' Bob's voice was low and his face was flushed.

'Hallo, Bob.' Connie's voice was equally low but her face was not flushed, it was extremely white.

'This—' Bob's hand went out to indicate Lizzie and in the second before he said, 'This is Elizabeth,' he thought, My God, what a situation! Her to come here and find me with Lizzie of all people. But in the next second he was in a measure relieved, for Connie, turning towards Lizzie and offering her hand, said, 'I've heard quite a lot about you,' and there was no double meaning in the remark.

'I'm glad to meet you.' Lizzie's voice was level and showed nothing of the agitation inside of her, but she swallowed and, looking towards the back of the retreating column, said hastily, 'I'll call Mike – he's just gone on with Mrs. Schofield.'

'Schofield? Lettice?' Now Connie turned to Bob and asked, 'Is it Lettice? Is she here?'

The red was fading somewhat from Bob's face and he gave a little smile now as he said, 'Yes, I'm afraid so.'

Lizzie, looking from one to the other, put in apologetically, 'She brought her daughter, she's one of Mary Ann's friends . . . it's Mary Ann's birthday party.'

'Yes, yes, I know.' Connie was now looking hard at Lizzie, and after a moment's hesitation she added, 'You . . . you were expecting me?'

There was just a fraction of a pause before Lizzie said, 'Yes, oh yes . . . yes, of course.' Her voice was slightly too loud and she went on now, too rapidly, 'Will you excuse me just a minute, I'll have to dash back to the house. I've just remembered I've left the kettle on for the tea – it'll be boiled dry.' Then just as she was about to hurry away she added,

'If you don't want to follow the cavalcade come back into the house. I'll run on, I'll – I'll see you in a minute.'

As Lizzie hurried back along the road to a kettle that didn't need seeing to she felt hot to the roots of her hair. Wait until she got hold of Mary Ann, she would skin her alive, she would; this was too much. And yet – she paused as she pushed open the garden gate and restrained herself from looking back along the road – you never knew what an unexpected meeting like this could bring about. But she shouldn't have done it; no, she shouldn't have done it. And now this would mean another one for tea and she hadn't enough cups. There were already two more than she had bargained for – she had to be prepared for Mr. Lord staying to tea, and then there was that Mrs. Schofield. She'd have to slip out the back way up to Ben's and ask him for the loan of some cups. . . .

Connie and Bob were standing exactly where Lizzie had left them. Connie's head was turned to one side and her eyes moved nervously about as she said in a low, strained voice, 'It's dreadful, she didn't expect me.'

'She didn't expect me, either.'

'No?' Connie's eyes came round to her husband's.

'No.' Bob wasn't sure of this, but he knew that if Connie thought he was in the same boat as herself she wouldn't feel so badly about it. He said now, 'Who gave you the invitation . . . Mary Ann?' His eyebrows moved up as he said the name.

'Yes, Mary Ann.'

'She gave me mine, too.' The corner of his mouth was pulled in. 'She's a terrible child is Mary Ann.'

The wary smile was wiped from Bob's lips as he saw Connie's eyes close tightly for a second and her hand press across her lips, and when turning quickly from him she muttered, 'I can't stay, make my apologies. Tell them I've had to . . .' he said rapidly and softly, 'Connie . . . Connie, don't go.' His hand was on her arm.

'I . . . I must; I can't stay here. It's . . . it's so embarrassing.'

'It needn't be, Connie. Connie, look at me.' His hand slipped down her arm until it reached her fingers, and as he clasped them her head fell forward and, the tears streaming down her face, she stammered, 'This . . . this is dreadful! I'll have to go, I must go.'

'Well, go this way.' He turned her about and led her in the direction of the house, and when they reached the hall he said softly, 'Come in here, there's no one in here.'

In the front room she dried her eyes while he stood close to her watching the process, and when she murmured, 'I feel dreadful, barging in like this', he knew that she was feeling dreadful not because she had barged in, but because of her meeting with him. He, too, was feeling dreadful . . . ghastly. He said softly, 'Forget it. Lizzie won't give it another thought; she's used to people coming and going.'

'She's nice . . . she's nice, Bob.' Connie was now looking at him. 'Different from what I expected, and – and she is rather beautiful.'

'Oh, damn Lizzie, look!' There was a moment during which they stood gazing at each other before his arms went round her and she fell against him, silent, and so, so thankful. . . .

Mike, just within the door of the kitchen, placed the three cups and saucers quietly on the dresser and, turning to Lizzie with wide twinkling eyes and exaggeratingly miming the words he had just heard, he said, 'Oh, damn Lizzie.'

Lizzie gave him an anything but gentle push before she went silently to the door leading into the hall and quietly closed it. Then, ignoring Bob's comment on her, she whispered, 'I'll skin that one alive.'

'Why?' Mike was whispering also.

'She planned all this, asking them both here today.'

'Well, hasn't it worked out? Damn Lizzie. Isn't that enough for you?'

'Oh, you!'

Mike grabbed at her arm and she said hastily, 'Now, now, Mike, stop it. Don't start any carry-on here, they're all coming back. And don't forget Mrs. Schofield, she expects you to give her all your attention.'

'Meow!' said Mike. Then, aiming at an impression of Bob's voice, he said, 'Damn Mrs. Schofield!' whereupon they both laughed softly.

'I'll make the tea now,' said Lizzie, 'and we'll get that over. Go and get them in. No, not that way.' She turned him about and pushed him in the direction of the back door, saying, 'You haven't much sense really.' And to this Mike replied, 'Well now, you couldn't expect me to, Liz, havin' passed it all on to me daughter.'

They were all seated at the table and it was proving a tight squeeze. Connie, now appearing as her suave, cool self, was seated between Mike and Bob, and across the table sat Mrs. Schofield between Mr. Lord and Tony. Mary Ann, on Mr. Lord's right, had the place of honour at the head of the table, and as she looked down its length over the colourful array of cakes and pyramids of sandwiches mounted with little flags to indicate what they were made of – an idea her mother had got out of a magazine – past the single-tiered birthday cake that dominated the centre of the table and with her name on it, right down the length of the board to where sat their Michael and Sarah Flannagan at the bottom, she thought that in a way it was fitting Sarah Flannagan should be here today to witness her wonderful party. She was seeing her surrounded by all her friends, her posh friends, for they were posh, you only had to listen to their voices; even when they were gabbling as they were doing now, talking and laughing all at once, they still sounded posh. Yes, it was fitting that Sarah had been allowed to witness this triumph. Yet it was strange but Mary Ann knew that she hadn't the feeling that should accompany this triumph. She knew how one should feel when they were triumphant, she had experienced triumph a number of times in her life, and today she should be over the moon with everything that had happened, because wasn't everything all right with everybody? With her ma and da. Oh yes, you only had to look at her ma and da to realize they were all right. And hadn't it worked out all right for Mr. Quinton and Mrs. Quinton? And Mr. Lord and Tony were all right again – that was a very good thing. And then there was that lovely, lovely pony. Oh, that pony. And their Michael was happy and she wasn't feeling nasty because it was Sarah Flannagan who had brought this about. But in spite of everything there was something missing. It was something that she would not think about, it was pushed to the back of her mind. She could, she knew, tell herself the one thing that was needed to make this day a day of light and wonder, to make this day a really outstanding, happy day, but she wouldn't say it. She became immersed in the babble of voices, the passing of cups, the handing of plates, the laughter. There was a lot of laughter; even Mr. Lord was laughing with his head back and his mouth open. Mrs. Schofield had achieved this. Tony was leaning across the table saying something funny to her da because her da's eyes were twinkling and he was wagging his hand at Tony. Mr. Quinton was talking and laughing with Mrs. Quinton, and Mrs. Quinton was looking at him with a look that told Mary Ann that it had been true what she had said, she liked him very much.

When the babble was at its highest, Roy Connor bent over the table and, looking up to the head of it, shouted, 'There's someone at the front door, someone knocking.' He must have had excellent hearing, for no one else seemed to have heard the knocking. And Mike called back, 'Well, let them come in then', and, raising his voice further, he cried, 'Come away in there . . .'

When his grannie wanted anyone to enter her house she cried, 'Come away in there,' and so Corny, hearing the remembered voice of Mike Shaughnessy calling above the noise from the room, 'Come away in there', pushed his trembling limbs forward and obeyed it. He walked from the front door, across the hall to the slightly open door of the kitchen and tentatively pushed it wide before taking one step inside the room.

It would be hard to imagine a more effective means of ensuring silence than Corny's appearance in the farm kitchen. No one could have looked more out of place and no one could have felt more out of place than he did. He had not known what to expect, he hadn't been able to visualize the party, Mary Ann's party. The parties they had at Christmas in their house consisted of a sing-song which got louder as the bottles of beer became fewer and which usually ended up in a fight if the whisky flowed too freely. So Corny had not been able to imagine anything like this room, or rather this table and the people seated round it, all, without exception, with their eyes fixed on him. It would be true to say that not one person at the table had been able to veil his surprise.

Lizzie was groaning to herself, 'Dear God. Oh, no . . . oh, what am I to do?' But she knew what she had to do, for in the next instance, when Mary Ann cried out on that high joy-filled note, she put her hand out swiftly and stopped her daughter from rising and dashing from the table.

As Lizzie's hand caught Mary Ann's arm Mr. Lord's came out on the other side of her, and she glanced from one to the other in surprise and startled indignation, and then looking towards the door she let out an agonized 'Oh!' for Corny was no longer there.

Then the eyes of Mary Ann, and not only Mary Ann but the whole company, turned to Mike, for, pushing his chair back briskly and rising to his feet, he strode swiftly towards the hall.

When Mike got on to the road Corny was well past the farm gate, and he hailed him, calling, 'Here a minute. Hi there!' But Corny took no notice, and when Mike saw the boy's step was on the verge of a run he sprinted over the distance between them. Coming up to the lad's side, he smiled easily as he asked, 'What's your hurry? Corny, isn't it, Corny Boyle? You remember me?'

Corny stood confronting Mike now, and after looking at him squarely for a moment his eyes swished away and he said, 'Aye, Aa remember you, Mr. Shaughnessy.'

'Well then, come on, come on back to the house.'

'No . . . no, Aa shouldn't a' come. . . . Aa knew Aa shouldn't a' come.'

'Why shouldn't you come? Mary Ann asked you, didn't she?'

'Aye she did, but Aa didn't think – Aa didn't think there'd be aall them there, them lads and lasses. An' that old bloke.' With a defiant glint in them now Corny brought his eyes back to Mike, and Mike, laughing, said, 'Oh, the old fellow

. . . Mr. Lord. Oh, you don't want to be afraid of him – his bark's much worse than his bite.'

'Aa'm not afraid of 'im. . . . Aa'm not afraid of neebody.' The shoulders went back and the chin out, and Mike, putting out his hand, touched the shoulder that was not much below his own and said quietly, 'That's the ticket, lad. As long as you speak the truth and owe no man nowt you needn't be afraid to face the Queen herself.'

Mike was now answering Corny in his own thick dialect, and when he said in an off-hand, easy way as if Corny's visit was an ordinary one, 'Come on, let's get in to tea,' Corny did not move. But his head drooped and his voice was not so arrogant now as he said, 'No, thanks aall the same, but Aa wouldn't get by with them lot. Aa knew Aa shouldn't a' come in the forst place, not in these togs anyhow. If it hadda been next week.' He stopped and his head moved slightly before saying, 'Me ma's gettin' me a new suit next week. She's gettin' a thirty pund club and havin' wor Bob, Harry and me aall rigged oot.'

There was something about this last statement that brought an odd feeling into Mike's throat: it was the feeling that had at times, when he was a lad, made him either hit out with his fists or seek some corner where he could cry unashamedly. He put out his one arm again and, gripping Corny by the shoulder, said roughly, 'Let's hear no more about clothes; it isn't clothes that make the chap. And one of these days you'll have more suits than you'll have pegs to put 'em on.'

Corny's head shot up and his eyes were bright and there was a look of amazement on his face as if he had heard a prophet speaking, and he said softly, 'Aye, Aa know, Aa've aallways told meself that. One day Aa'll have ten suits and everythin' Aa want. Funny you sayin' that.' A smile touched his face now and Mike laughed and turned him slowly about as he lied, or let it be said, as he told a tale, for was he not Mary Ann's father. 'I'm a bit of a fortune-teller meself,' he said. 'A better name for it would be character-reader. I can generally tell what a bloke is made of and what he's coming to.'

'Can ya?' Corny was relaxed for a moment; he was looking up admiringly at Mr. Shaughnessy – Mike Shaughnessy – whom he remembered having seen rolling drunk and dancing in the street and who now looked . . . well, like as if he was rich.

'Aye,' said Mike – he was walking slowly and casually towards the gate. 'You remember the fellow you saw driving the car the other day with the old 'un?' As he felt Corny's shoulder stiffen he added, 'Oh, he's all right. That's Tony; he's the old fellow's grandson. They didn't discover the relationship until three years ago. The old man hasn't had the chance to alter him. Tony's all right, you'll like Tony.'

'He sent me some things.' Corny's voice was low now and he looked at his feet as he walked. 'And I wouldn't hev 'em.'

'Oh, I don't blame you.' Mike's voice was airy. 'But mind you—' He paused slightly in his step. 'Tony would mean no offence, his only aim was to give you a hand.'

'Aye p'raps. But, aall the same, Aa'm not startin' on second-hand togs, Aa swore Aa wouldn't. Ye see, me ma's always told me about me granny and . . .'

'Aah!' Mike cut in. 'There's a woman, your granny. You know, Fanny's the best friend I've got. Ah, here we are. Get yourself in there.' He pushed Corny slightly forward, and kept pressing him until they entered the kitchen. And with his voice on a high airy note he cried, 'Is there any room up at the top there? Ah, yes, move along, Mary Ann. Is there a chair, Liz? . . . By the way, this is a friend of mine.' He put his arm around Corny's shoulder as he surveyed the company. 'We can't go into individual introductions at the moment, there's too many of us, but you just call him Corny, short for Cornelius . . . eh?' He gave Corny a little hug, then added, 'You'll get to know everybody by and by. Come on, let's get on with this tea.'

Mary Ann's heart was thumping under her ribs, and for the first time today she had that jumping, joyous feeling inside of her. She ignored the subdued quietness that had settled on the table; she ignored the terrible look on Mr. Lord's face; she ignored her mother's stiff countenance; she ignored the polite, surprised look on the faces of her two best friends and was about to smooth matters in her own way when her da caused the silence to break on tentative laughter when he exclaimed loudly, 'Put your bugle down, lad. You're not going to drink your tea through that, are you?'

Mary Ann, eagerly taking the instrument from Corny's hand and laughing high in her head, cried, 'Oh, Da! It isn't a bugle, it's a cornet, and Corny's a smashing player.' There was more laughter, a little louder this time, but still lacking the unrestrained quality that had pervaded the party before Corny's arrival. For the moment the company seemed to be dominated by the feelings of both Lizzie and Mr. Lord, which were vividly expressed in their faces. And then Mrs. Schofield spoke and she addressed herself directly to Corny. 'I have a brother who plays the cornet,' she said.

'Hev ya?'

On the sound of 'Hev ya?' Lizzie lowered her eyes. Up to this moment she would have said of herself that she was no upstart, but now she admitted quite frankly that all her feelings were those of an upstart, for she was ashamed that she or anyone belonging to her had ever been in such circumstances as would oblige them to make even the acquaintance of anyone like Corny Boyle. Oh, she wished him far away, anywhere but here . . . 'Hev ya?' Oh, Mary Ann! What was to be done with her? It was true what Mr. Lord said, she had no sense of correct behaviour, she would never have mixed her invitations to this drastic extent if she had. Of all the children she could have invited from the district round Mulhattan's Hall, Corny Boyle was the roughest customer. It wouldn't have been so bad if he had come at any other time, but now, when she was surrounded by . . . these others. Lizzie refrained from giving Mary Ann's posh friends any class status. And there was Mr. Lord; he was livid. Oh, what would the outcome of this be? The party was spoiled, couldn't Mary Ann realize that – for doubtless 'hev ya?' was just the beginning.

She looked at her daughter, but Mary Ann was engrossed at the moment in what Mrs. Schofield was saying to Corny.

'Yes, and he drove us nearly round the bend; in fact, as the saying goes, up the wall and over the other side. And I was the first one over.' Mrs. Schofield cast her deep blue eyes round the table now and caught the laughter to her, then went on, 'Of course, that was when he was learning, but now when he can play, well he hardly ever touches it. It'll be the same with you.' She looked back to Corny.

'Noo . . . noo, it won't. Aa'm gonna larn it proper. A man near us is larning me now.'

'Well, good for you. You'll have to play something to us after tea, eh?'

'Aye . . . aye, Aa will.' Corny was looking directly at Mrs. Schofield, and to do this he had to cut his glance from Mr. Lord who was at her elbow.

'Perhaps you'll give me a lesson,' said Mrs. Schofield, still talking to Corny. 'I feel I've missed something in not taking advantage of our Robert. It mustn't sound so bad when you're doing the blowing and not just listening. What do you say?' She turned her eyes for the fraction of a second on Mr. Lord, and before he had time to make any caustic comment she flashed her laughing gaze round the table again, crying, 'We'll have a percussion band. You, Mary Ann, you can play the comb. And you, Beatrice, we'll give you a tray. And Janice, you can bang two loaf tins. And Tony there can . . .'

Mike looked across the table at this woman who was allotting household instruments to everyone at the table, and the smile deepened on his face as he thought to himself: I made a mistake; now I know why men marry such women. She's no fool, that one, and she's kind with it for all her dithery lah-de-dah. Aye, she is that. He took up the ball she had set rolling and cried, 'What would you give me?'

'Oh, now, let's see.' She appealed to the whole table. 'What shall we give him?'

There were cries of this and that, and when Connie to the side of him said, 'I'd give him a wash-board,' he turned to her, laughing. 'All right,' he said, 'and wait till you hear me; a wash-board it will be.'

Everybody had made a suggestion for the percussion band with the exception of Lizzie and Mr. Lord. Lizzie now handed Corny a cup of tea for which, after looking hard at her, he said 'Ta', and then almost before he had laid the cup on the table he made an impatient exclamation to himself and, putting his hand in his pocket, he pulled out what appeared to be a stick of thumb thickness, about nine inches in length, wrapped in newspaper, and for the first time since coming to the table and sitting next to Mary Ann he turned and looked at her and spoke. 'That's for yer birthday,' he said.

'Oh . . . oh, thanks, Corny.' She hadn't the foggiest notion what was under the paper, and for a moment she hesitated to open it in fear that it would be something that might bring derision on the giver. Slowly she unfolded the wrapping, and when the thing lay across her hand there was a gasp of surprise from those nearest to her, for Corny's present was a small flute cut out of black ebony and inlaid between the stops with mother-of-pearl. It was of exquisite workmanship and delicate beauty, and that it should have been given by this rough lump of a lad seemed to add to its lustre.

'Oh, isn't it beautiful!' Connie was leaning forward across the table, and Mrs. Schofield, bending forward too, exclaimed, 'Oh, that is lovely.'

Speaking to Corny for the first time, Tony asked quietly, 'Where did you come across that?'

'Aa picked it up in a junk shop.'

He picked it up in a junk shop. Mike was repeating the words to himself. This unprepossessing lump of humanity – for even Mike couldn't in any way glamorize Corny, this lad who had been brought up in the low end of Howden, who had never experienced any of the niceties of life – had . . . picked out from among junk this instrument of beauty. He himself was no musician. He could dig away at the piano by ear and he could sing a bit, but he knew nothing about musical instruments, yet he did know that the flute, or whatever it was, was a little miracle of workmanship.

'Oh, Corny!' Mary Ann's lips were trembling, perhaps a little with relief but mostly with happiness. Of all the presents she had had today, and she'd had a lot, this was the best. Nor had she forgotten the pony. She looked up at Corny, and although her voice was low it brought a hush to the table. 'I'll learn to play it, Corny. Yes, I will. I promise I'll learn to play it.'

'Between homework and riding lessons?'

She flashed a quick look over her shoulder towards Mr. Lord. His voice was even and controlled but it did not deceive her; she knew he was vexed, even mad, but that did not stop her from saying, 'Yes, yes, I'll fit it in some way, but I'll learn it.' She flashed her laughing face up at her mother now and said, 'I'll play it in bed, Ma.' In her excitement she had forgotten that for today her ma also was not her ma but her mother.

Mr. Lord looked down at his plate and applied himself to crumbling up a piece of cake. He was hurt, deeply hurt, and angry. Angry at himself for being angry, for allowing this child to retain the power to hurt him. He had given her the pony for her birthday present, for he knew that nobody else would be able to give her such a present, even if they had thought of it, and she had been overjoyed with the pony, but neither the animal nor himself had elicited from her the feeling which she was bestowing on this . . . penny-whistle, gormless, uncouth individual. What had he said to him? 'By God! I'll get on.' He glanced at the boy now. He was drinking his tea, likely with loud sucking sounds if it was possible to hear him.

Just as Mr. Lord was twitching his eye back to his plate again, Corny, from over the rim of his cup, looked at the old man and, catching his disparaging glance on himself, returned it unblinkingly. It was Mr. Lord who looked away first.

If that boy had entry into this house, and there was every likelihood that he would, following on Shaughnessy's attitude, then the child would be influenced by him. How old was he . . . sixteen or so? He would have to do some thinking about this and step warily. It was a pity, he thought now, that he had already exchanged words with him; he could do much more to nip this thing in the bud had he approached the youth from a different angle. There was one thing sure: he must make it his business to get this boy away from the vicinity by some means, either fair or foul. He was certainly not going to have his schemes brought to nothing by a lump of a lout like this. No, he certainly was not. He more than surprised Tony by turning to him at this juncture and saying, in a tone which by a stretch could be termed jocular, 'Why haven't you learned some musical instrument?'

'What! Me?' Tony's eyes were wide as he looked at his grandfather, but he was not deceived by the old man's change of front, for he knew he was furious at the boy's intrusion, but he replied with a laugh, 'I'm tone deaf, you know I am; I can't even sing in the bath. Don't forget you've complained of the noise more than once.'

After this exchange, Tony's and Mike's glances, meeting quietly across the table, said: 'The old boy's not going to lie down under this.'

The tea lasted much longer than Lizzie had anticipated, and although she herself was not feeling at ease she was glad to see that the company had apparently forgotten Corny's presence – that is, all except Mary Ann. She would have to talk to Mary Ann later tonight or perhaps tomorrow. She would have to tell her, in a quiet way, that you didn't look at people as she was doing at Corny, even if you liked the person, and that if she wanted to keep anybody's affection – and God forbid that she would ever want to keep this boy's – she must hide her feelings, and for a long, long time. There were lots of things she must talk to her about – she was thirteen now. Oh dear! dear! Why had this boy put his nose in the door today, today of all days, when everything was going so beautifully?

Lizzie now gave Mary Ann a slight dig in the side which had the two-fold purpose of drawing her attention away from Corny and giving her the signal that she and the younger members could leave the table. But apparently the older members wanted to leave the table, too, and there was a general outpouring into the sunshine and on to the lawn again. But not with the instruments of the percussion band. The talk about that had served the purpose Mrs. Schofield had intended.

Corny kept very much in the rear of the company and for the short time she was allowed Mary Ann stayed by his side. She was happy. This was the most wonderful party she had ever had and, oh, she was going to learn to play the flute. It was a beautiful flute, everybody thought so. It was the nicest present she had received today – or at any other time. Well, there was the pony. But that was different somehow. Mr. Lord had been mad at Corny coming. That was at the beginning; he didn't seem so bad now, he was with Mrs. Schofield. Mrs. Schofield was a funny woman, but she did make people laugh. She was making them laugh now. On the sound of the laughter she deluded herself that everybody was enjoying themselves and there was no need for her to bother and she could spent the rest of the time with Corny.

Looking up at him now, she said with bald diplomacy, 'You needn't go when the others do, need you, because you came late. If you'll stay I'll show you round the farm and take you up to see my pony. Oh, he's lovely.'

'Did ya da gie you it?'

'No . . .' She paused before the admission. 'It was Mr. Lord.'

'Oh, him. He doosn't like me.'

'Oh, but he will in a little while; he's like that with everybody to start with. Oh' – it was a loud 'oh' – 'he was worse than that with me. He even told Ben, that's his servant, to throw me out of his house.'

'He did?'

'Yes, he did.'

'Mary Ann!'

Mary Ann turned to find her mother looking at her.

'You must see to your guests and play some games.' As Lizzie said this she gave Corny a weak smile, and Corny, understanding, stood stock still.

'I won't be a minute.' Mary Ann reassured Corny before reluctantly leaving him to join Beatrice and the rest. She did not say, 'Come along and join in' – she couldn't imagine Corny playing, not at their games, anyway.

As Corny found himself looking at Lizzie he felt as he had done when he first entered the kitchen, and once again he said, but under his breath, 'Aa shouldn't a' come, should Aa?'

'Don't be silly, Corny, of course you should; you're very welcome.' Lizzie was surprised at the enthusiasm she put into this comforting but untrue statement.

He said now, 'Me Gran will go off the deep end when she knaws.'

'Why should she?' Lizzie found she was saying all the things she didn't mean, for were she in Fanny's place she'd find more than enough to go off the deep end about.

She was wondering in her mind what to say to him next when the situation was saved by Mrs. Schofield crying, 'Oh, there you are. Now come on, play the cornet, and something jolly, mind, nothing highfalutin.'

'Aw, Aa couldn't play anythin' high flootin' if Aa tried.'

Corny was laughing now, and Lizzie found herself being amazed at the fact that this dizzy woman could put this lump of a lad at his ease, whereas she herself, who was, she felt, an understanding, sensible type, put him on edge. But then, wasn't she Mary Ann's mother? Mrs. Schofield had nothing to lose with Corny.

'Ya reely want ta hear it?'

'Of course I do, everybody does. Listen, everybody.' She stopped and flung her arm upwards as if she was mistress of ceremonies. 'Squat a minute, Corny's going to play.'

'Oh, Lord!' It was the boy Roy Connor speaking from where he stood at the bottom of the lawn among his friends. 'This'll be Corny by name and Corny by cornet.' The witticism brought sniggers from the girls and guffaws from the boys, until a voice said, 'Connor!' It was the voice of the fifth-former speaking to a second-form grub, and the grub reacted without remembering that he wasn't at school and said humbly, 'Yes, Shaughnessy?'

'We'll have none of that.'

'No, Shaughnessy.'

In this moment Mary Ann loved their Michael and she told herself that she would never, never, never be nasty to him again. It was in this moment, too, that the first stirrings of love flickered in Sarah Flannagan's breast for Michael Shaughnessy. She had liked Michael, she had always liked him, she had always been attracted by him, mostly it must be said, because of the halo of the Grammar School. But it was now that the liking changed to the first spark of rare love, and thereby Michael Shaughnessy's and Sarah Flannagan's destinies were entwined, painfully entwined. But as yet they did not know this and were ecstatically happy on this afternoon of the party.

'Quiet now . . . quiet.' Mrs. Schofield was now flapping her hands wildly, and her daughter, in shamed tones, whispered to Mary Ann, 'Oh, Mary Ann, I'm sorry. Oh, I hate it when Mummy takes control and acts the goat; oh, I am sorry.'

Mary Ann, glancing for a moment at Janice, suddenly realized that you could be ashamed of your people for other things besides drink. It was a very comforting thought, a very comforting thought indeed. Anyway, she couldn't now see much about Mrs. Schofield to be ashamed of, but nevertheless Janice was ashamed and deeply. Remembering the technique of Mrs. McBride in praising her da when she herself needed comfort on his behalf, she turned to her friend and said, 'I think your mother's lovely.'

'You do?'

'Yes . . . yes, I do. And she's a sport. And I think you're awful for saying that.'

'Quiet, you grown-ups.' Mrs. Schofield was now silencing Connie and Bob and Mike with more flaps of her hands. She disregarded the fact that they were speaking to Mr. Lord. 'Now, there you are, they've all stopped talking. Now play, Corny.'

Before Corny lifted the cornet to his mouth he looked at Mrs. Schofield and smiled. It was a broad smile and changed his face completely.

Nobody seemed to recognize the piece Corny was playing, but what the elders did recognize was that the notes were true and unblurred and that the boy, holding the cornet pointing skywards, had completely lost his self-consciousness and become an entirely new being. His coat sleeves had slid down almost to his elbows, but this did not make him appear ludicrous; it was the player who was to the fore now. Mike, as he listened, thought, 'Aye, and he might an' all have more suits than pegs to put them on – this is the age of the cornet and such noises. He might have been born at the right time, who knows?'

When Corny stopped there was loud clapping, and when it ceased he said, 'That was me own piece, Aa made it up.' And then with an unselfconscious twinkle, said, 'D'ya know this?' And he had reached only the third note when there were scornful cries and laughs of, 'Oh, Blaydon Races!' but before he had finished it there was only one person on the lawn who wasn't singing, and that was Mr. Lord.

Lizzie was in the kitchen clearing away and she was not a little amazed when she heard the singing, and perhaps a little relieved, but a few minutes later, when she came into the hall and looked on to the back of the player where he stood in front of the open doorway, she once again closed her eyes and lowered her head, for the tune he had started was being picked up by Mike and his clear deep tones were ringing across the lawn, accompanied by the laughing treble of Mary Ann. They were singing, 'He stands at the corner and whistles me out'. And the climax came with a great roar of laughter when a cow in the byre set up a loud moo-ing. Then everybody was singing, 'He stands at the corner and whistles me out, With his hands in his pockets, and his shirt hanging out.'

Again it was only Mr. Lord who didn't joint in; again it was only his face that wasn't cracking with laughter. He stands at the corner and whistles me out! He could see Mary Ann singing and gambolling with the lamb as she sang this song, and there she was now yelling her head off, sanctioned this time by her father. Well, he mustn't worry, things had worked out for him in the past; he hadn't the slightest doubt but that they would work his way again. Undoubtedly, it would need greater effort, but then all things worth while needed effort.

And he began right away on the effort when Corny finished playing. In clear tones he spoke to him across the space that divided them, saying, 'I think, young man, that you'll make something of that instrument before you're finished.'

Corny stared at the old man, not able to believe that he was speaking to him, and in a tone of praise. But he was wary, on his guard, and he made no reply. When a few minutes later the old man walked casually to his side and said, 'Tell me, what do you intend to make of yourself?' he looked at him for a long while before answering, and then his tone was gruff and dull, 'Aa'm gonna be a cornet player.'

'How are you going to eat until you become a professional cornet player?'

It was a sensible question and Corny gave it a sensible answer. 'Aa'm goin' in a garrage forst,' he said.

'Ah, a garage. You're interested in cars, then?'

'Aye, Aa am.' Corny's tone could have been interpreted as: make what you like of that.

At this point Mike stopped Mary Ann from going to Corny and claiming his attention, and as he watched the old man and the lad talking he thought, The old boy's up to something; but, anyway, if the lad gets talking he'll find he's no fool and he'll forget his suit and see the makings of him.

But Tony, looking at his grandfather talking to the boy, just thought, Poor devil. What chance does he stand? . . .

It was about seven-thirty when the cars began to arrive. The party was at an end. Of all the farewells the high peak was the waving away of Mrs. Schofield, and the last words Mike said to her were, 'Bless you', and she laughed up into his face from the car wheel and said, 'Bless you, too, Mike. And don't think you've seen the last of me, for I'm coming again, invitation or no.' Lizzie, too, laughed at this woman. In spite of her dizziness she felt that she liked her. Anyway, she had certainly eased a nasty situation.

There was more laughter when Mrs. Schofield's car once again got into a tangle with Jane Willoughby's outside the front gate. Jane was in a bad temper, for on the sight of her cousin Connie all compatible again with Bob, she felt she must have missed a great deal by not making an effort and staying to tea.

Bob had already helped his wife into his car before going round to take his seat at the wheel, and now there was Lizzie on his side and Mike and Mary Ann on Connie's to say good-bye. Connie's last words were for Mary Ann. 'I wouldn't have missed your party for anything, Mary Ann,' she said.

Mary Ann could say nothing, she could only smile from one to the other in turn as she hung on to her da's hand – the Quintons were kind again and were no longer a menace to her family, so that was that.

It was when the last car had gone, the last farewell had been said, that Tony, touching Mike's arm and drawing him slightly aside, motioned with his head to where Mr. Lord was still sitting talking to Corny, an apparently enraptured Corny now. And Tony with a quizzical smile on his face said, under his breath, 'You'd never believe that he could get going so quickly but he has already disposed of the boy.'

'Disposed? What do you mean?'

'He's got him interested in America and cars.'

'But what's that got to do with disposing of him?'

'Can't you see, Mike? Oh, but perhaps you don't know. He's got connections who have a car business in America and he holds more than a few shares in the concern. I've been listening to him working.' Tony laughed. 'He's told the lad he can get him set on there.'

'But why? What does he want to do that for? He looked as if he hated the lad's guts when he came into the kitchen.'

'Oh, be yourself, Mike,' Tony laughed. 'Where are your wits? Can't you see he's making my path clear by removing an obstacle. And from your daughter's show of interest in our musician he's definitely going to be an obstacle. Don't you get it?'

Mike looked at Tony in silence for a moment. He was relieved and glad that he was seeing the business now with an amusing slant and he shook his head as he murmured, 'Well, well. Can you beat it? He's simply amazing. But look . . .' He nodded over his shoulder. 'Look there. Somehow I don't think we need concern ourselves overmuch about Corny being drafted to America, do you?'

Mary Ann was running up the garden towards Corny and Mr. Lord. Everybody had gone now; she could have Corny to herself; she was going to take him round the farm and Mr. Lord wouldn't mind. For Mr. Lord liked Corny, he had talked to him for the last hour – she wouldn't have believed it, not after what happened in the street that day. She came to a stop at Mr. Lord's knee and cried, 'Hasn't it been a lovely party, Mr. Lord? Hasn't it been wonderful?' Then before Mr. Lord could say anything she grabbed Corny's arm and cried, 'Come on and see my pony. Mr. Lord gave it to me for my birthday present – didn't you?' She leant towards the old man and put her hand affectionately on his lapel, and for an instant he placed his own wrinkled, blue-veined one on top of it, but he said nothing; he just watched her hurry away, with the gangling boy at her side. As the ill-assorted pair passed Mike and Tony at the gate Mike stretched out his hand and said to Corny, 'You'd better leave that with me. If you start blowing that up in the fields you'll scare the wits out of the cattle.' Corny, without hesitation, handed his beloved cornet to Mike, then with his head not bowed and his limbs not so gangling he looked ahead and struck out down the road, Mary Ann at his side.

But now she was not hitching and skipping as was usual with her when she was happy, for like an unexpected blow it had come to her that her hitching days were over. It was at the moment that Corny had handed the instrument to Mike that it happened. It was as if her da had recognized that Corny was to be her lad, and approved. In this moment of awakening she also realized, and fully, that he was the only one who did approve. She knew, too, that she had been daft to imagine that Mr. Lord was talking to Corny because he liked him. She asked now in a sober tone : 'What were you and Mr. Lord talking about?'

'Cars.'

'Cars?'

'Aye, cars.' Corny cast a sidelong glance down on her, and she saw that he was amused and that he was surprisingly at his ease. He was no longer on the defensive. 'American ones.'

'Oh!'

'He's got a say in some works oot there.'

'In America?'

'Aye.' He walked steadily on, looking ahead. 'He's for hevin' me set on.'

'In America!' Her voice was high.

They had just turned into the farmyard gate. They stopped and looked at each other.

'But . . . but you can get work in a garage here – in England.'

'Aye . . . aye, Aa knaw that, but he wants ta pack me off to America.'

'But why?'

'To get rid of me cos'.'

As they continued to stare at each other Mary Ann's feelings became a mixture of fear, misery, and disappointment. Then these emotions were swiftly engulfed by a surge of indignation. . . . That was why Mr. Lord had been kind to Corny. Oh! . . . Oh!

'Are you going?'

'Well—' Corny pulled on his ear and, as he did so, he turned his head and looked about the farm-yard, saying quietly, 'There's one thing sartin: Aa'll nivver git a chance like this agen. It could set me up. This could be it. Aa aallways knew Aa'd git me chance one day.'

'Oh, but, Corny . . .'

The wonder of the day had vanished and Corny did not seem to hear her appeal, for he went on looking about him and talking. 'Aa could take it 'cos he doesn't knaw Aa'm on ta him – he thinks Aa swallowed it. He's not very bright up top or he wouldn't uv changed his tune so quickly an' laid it on see thick.'

With a sudden pull on his arm she drew his attention back to her. 'I know why he wants to send you to America.'

'Aye, so div Aa.'

Her eyes became so large that her face looked even smaller in contrast.

'It's to stop me an' you dunchin' inta each other. Me granny told me a while since what he's got on the cards for you, an' he's got the idea Aa might muck it up.' There followed a pause, then, 'De ya want me ta gan t'America?'

'No, oh no. No, I don't.' In the look on her face and the intensity of her words, she was exposing her vital weakness to Corny. A weakness that amounted almost to a flaw in her character, for where she loved she could not lie. Her feelings would always present her as a target. She was fortunate that Corny's interior was in direct contrast to his outward appearance, for there was neither arrogance nor roughness in his manner as he said, 'Well then, Aa won't.'

The heaviness left her body and for a second she had a desire to jump, but she checked it, and found she had to take three quick steps, for Corny had resumed his walk again.

'Yer da's fer me.'

Mary Ann's whole face was bright; her great eyes were shining as with triumph as she answered, 'Yes, yes. I know.'

'Yer ma's not though.'

'She will be.'

'No, no, she won't. Aa divvn't taalk nice enough for hor.'

'Oh, Corny, I'll learn . . . teach you. I will.' She half stopped, but he carried on, his big feet hitting the ground flatly with each step. 'Divint knaw as Aa want ta talk different. Any road, Aa won't hev time, workin' an arl that.'

When she made no comment he glanced sideways at her and remarked, 'Not less Aa come oot here a night or so a week.'

'Yes, yes, you could do that.' She was eager again.

'Aye.' He seemed to consider. 'Aye, Aa could de that.'

'Yes, yes, I could do that.'

'What?'

'Just what you said: "Aye, aye, Aa could de that".' She smiled gently at him. 'Say "Yes, yes, I could do that". That's your first lesson.'

'Aw !' He put his head back and laughed.

'Go on, say it.'

'Aw, no man.'

'Go on.'

'Aw well ! . . . Yes, yes, Aa could do that.'

The translation was too much for them both, for they began to laugh. They laughed and they laughed. Then Mary Ann, grabbing at his hand, compelled him to run with her. And he suited his steps to hers as he was always to do.

When the sound of the laughter floated down over the garden it carried no indication that a boy's life had been taken in hand, or that Mary Ann's destiny was already cut to a complicated pattern, and certainly not that the owner of the deep laugh had just managed a translation from thick Geordie into northern accented English.

Then the laughter was abruptly cut off and replaced by the strains of a song.

As he listened Mike's face widened into a smile, but Lizzie's face had a neutral look. The effect of the sound on Mr. Lord was to make him close his eyes.

The breeze, seeming to catch Mary Ann's voice and separate it from her partner's, bore it down to the garden, and the words hung on the air:

'Still I love him, can't deny it.
I'll be with him, wherever he goes.'

Also by CATHERINE COOKSON:

THE INVITATION

When the Gallachers received an invitation from the Duke of Moorshire to attend his musical evening, Maggie was overwhelmed. Naturally, she did not see the invitation as the rock on which she was to perish; nor was she prepared for the reactions of her family. However, Maggie herself was to be the prime mover of the downfall of the family she loved too dearly . . .

0 552 09035 2   35p

THE MENAGERIE

The Broadhursts were a mining family and they appeared to be happy, united, and loyal.

But it was only Jinny – wife, mother, sister – who held the Broadhursts together with a pride and strength that prevented their fears and hates from overwhelming them. There was Jack her younger son; Lottie, her sister who was not quite . . . normal; and Larry the bright one, her favourite, who was obsessed with the memory of the girl who had jilted him and who would sacrifice anyone, family and friends alike, if he could only see Pam Turnbull again . . .

0 552 08653 3   30p

THE LONG CORRIDOR

To outsiders the life of Dr. Paul Higgins appeared to be a contented one. He seemed to have everything a man could want. But the façade that Paul and Bett Higgins presented to the world concealed a welter of hate that grew worse with the passing years.

Between Paul and Bett stood the barrier of the past – of secrets that, were they known, could affect everyone about them . . .

0 552 08493 X   25p

Other fine novels appearing in Corgi include:

By R. F. DELDERFIELD

THERE WAS A FAIR MAID DWELLING
THE UNJUST SKIES

While complete in themselves, these two novels tell the story of John Leigh and Diana Gayelorde-Sutton; the first, set in beautiful Devonshire, relates their meeting and subsequent love-affair; the second, in a more international setting during the Second World War.

Circumstances have separated John and Diana who is now married to Yves De Royden, the cold son of a French tycoon; and John is established in a life of quiet companionship with his wife, Alison. But Alison is killed in an air-raid, and John, who had previously been with the R.A.F. is persuaded to work for the French Resistance. Only to find that one of his colleagues in the movement is – Diana . . .

0 552 08702 5   35p   0 552 08753 X   35p

DAY OF THE DANCING SUN by PHYLLIS HASTINGS, author of ALL EARTH TO LOVE

Will and Caroline Dyke had forged a dynasty between them – a family of sons and daughters bred on the farming land of the Sussex hills.

Caroline had been a vibrant and rebellious girl and now as the indomitable matriarch of her tribe, she found herself faced with a family whose loves and hates were as strong as her own. So when Peregrine Dyke brings home a young wife, it becomes a signal for family life to erupt once more into a sequence of violent and passionate events . . .

0 552 08754 8   35p

THE WINNERS by JAMES MITCHELL

The dinner party was a reunion for the successful ones: Laidlaw, the host, galloping towards his first million; Moulton, the brilliant physicist; Arnott, the eminent and well-married doctor; Fitzgerald, the painter. These four had attended the same provincial grammar school – and had made it. It was going to be an evening of social triumph – or was it?

Laidlaw knew one of his guests was about to be demolished – and was enjoying the prospect . . .

0 552 08996 6   40p

A selected list of fine novels that appear in Corgi: